The Empath's Lover

Sidonie Savage

Ternias Publishing

Contents

For permission requests, contact:
Sidonie Savage /Ternias Publishing.
Sydney / Nova Scotia, B1P 7H3
www.sidoniesavage.com / www.terniaspublishing.com

The story, all names, characters, and incidents portrayed in this production are fictitious. No identification with actual persons (living or deceased), places, buildings, and products is intended or should be inferred.

The Empath's Lover / Sidonie Savage. —2nd edition 2023
ISBN (eBook): 978-1-989383-05-6
ISBN (Paperback): 978-1-989383-06-3

Preface

Disclaimer

The Empath's Lover is a Science Fiction M/M (male/male) Romance Novella. Due to adult language and themes, it is intended for readers ages 18+.

A Note from the Author

For the scenes where Tulq'on thinks or speaks, you will notice differences in the register of the language. This is intentional. For example, when he thinks or interacts with his own kind, the language level is more sophisticated, as it is supposed to represent his native language. For the scenes where he is "speaking" English, the language is more awkward as English is not his native language.

One

Awakening

DAVON

I'm not certain what it was that registered first in my consciousness: my incessant shivering and the chattering of my teeth, or the irritating beeps followed by the hiss of a pressure lock disengaging. Maybe I noticed them all at the same time. I opened my eyes slowly. It took me a few minutes more to remember who I was, where, and why.

My name is Davon Pax. I'm Chief Medical Officer and Microbiologist on-board the Explorer 2. I repeated the information to myself to try to clear the fog from my brain.

If everything had gone as it should, we would be on approach to Neptune and its moons. I would have to verify that to say with total certainty, but that was where we were supposed to be awakened.

I sat up slowly to give my body time to adjust before swinging my legs over the side of the cryo-chamber. I braced myself against it before attempting to stand on my own two feet. Once I felt steady enough, I reached into my small locker, located just to the side of the cryo-unit, to grab a thermal blanket to warm up before getting dressed. As my eyes adjusted to the light, I looked around the room to try to reorient myself.

"How are you feeling, Doc?" asked a sleepy voice off to my right a few minutes later.

"Captain Boyton." I nodded in greeting as I shrugged on my lab coat. "I'm feeling fine. No side effects we didn't expect. Don't attempt to stand yet," I added when he looked like he was going to get up. "Let me look you over first." I grabbed the vitals scanner and made my way to him. As I took the last of his readings, I heard the hiss of another cryo-unit opening to my right.

We were woken in a specific order, of course—everything about this mission had been planned to the last detail. I was first since I would check everyone over as they exited their units. Captain Asher Boyton, our pilot and lead engineer, followed. Then there was Valria Ledoux, our astronomer, astrophysicist, and cosmologist. Sylas Hayes—our chemist, physicist, mechanic, and co-pilot—liked to tease her that she had three PhDs in the same subject. Finally, there was Tira Massey, our botanist, nutritionist, and physiologist.

I had just finished with Ledoux and was attaching the equipment to Hayes when he spoke. "Hey Doc. Did you miss me?"

I glanced up at him and sure enough, he was wearing his flirty grin.

"I know it's been a decade, Hayes, but for some strange reason it feels like only yesterday that I saw you last," I quipped. "So, no, I didn't miss you."

He chuckled and looked around the room as I continued my check-up.

"You know," he said, "this kind of reminds me of that movie I saw where the heroine wakes up from cryo-sleep only to find out—"

"I don't want to know, Hayes," I interrupted. "For the life of me, I'll never understand why you'd want to be an astronaut after watching all those space-alien horror movies you're obsessed with."

He shrugged. "What can I say, I love space, and I'm a bit of an adrenaline junkie. Plus, they're classics."

"Why not go sky-diving or something if you're looking for a jolt of adrenaline? Why watch movies where space monsters try to destroy the human race? Are you trying to psyche yourself out?"

"Eh, it doesn't hurt to be mentally prepared for the worse."

"Yeah, well, I'd rather hope for the best. I mean, if we did encounter other intelligent life out here, it would be a shame if we jumped to conclusions and started an interstellar war when they just wanted to say hello."

He shrugged again. "I guess I can see your point."

"Okay, you're done. You can go get dressed and get something to eat."

"I don't know, Doc. I'm feeling kind of weak. Are you sure you can't help me take off my cryo-suit?" Like everyone else, he had only pulled it down to his waist—just far enough for me to check his vitals.

"Knock it off, Hayes," I said. I turned my back to him and approached Massey to check her out. I would have to check their vitals at regular intervals for the first day to see how their bodies were adjusting. This was the longest time humans had ever been in cryo-sleep and one of my many jobs was to gather and track the data to see if there were any negative effects to prolonged use.

❦ ♥ ❦ ♥ ❦

By the time I was done, Boyton was sitting in front of our main computer terminal just finishing up his status update to mission control back on Earth. Ledoux sat next to him, I assumed confirming that everything was as it was supposed to be.

"How does everything look?" I asked as I approached.

"Great," Boyton said. He rubbed his eyes.

"Look at this data from when we passed Jupiter," Ledoux chimed in. Her voice was chipper and excited when compared to Boyton, who seemed as though he hadn't quite woken up from the cryo-sleep yet.

I placed my hand on her shoulder and gave a gentle squeeze. "Why don't you tell the whole crew about it in a bit. We should still be a couple of hours out from orbit. I'm sure everyone is anxious to check the data, but we should eat and give our bodies time to adjust." Just in case she or Boyton needed extra incentive, I jerked my head in the direction of the others. "They're still groggy from cryo-sleep. I'm sure you must be too."

Captain Boyton glanced over at them with a look of concern. "Yeah, you're right. Let's go."

We gathered in the small room that passed as a mess hall. It wasn't large or fancy, but it got the job done. The room also had one of the few windows with a view to the outside. Most of our navigation was done by sensors and computers, leaving the hull with as few vulnerabilities as possible, like windows. It made sense, I knew, but I still wished we had more of a view of the marvels we were no doubt passing by, even at this very moment.

I walked over to the little window and leaned to the left so I could watch the rings that spun around the exterior of the ship, a low hum all that could be heard of their movement from inside. They were what created gravity in the Explorer 2. No more floating around weightlessly like the first space pioneers of over a hundred years ago, thankfully. We'd practiced in zero-gravity chambers, of course, for times when we might need it, but I was never very fond of it.

Massey walked over and slapped a ration package into my palm. "Here you go, Doc. Did you check your own vitals?"

"Of course," I said with a smile. "I knew you'd give me hell if I didn't."

She was a sweet girl. Even during our long hours of training back on Earth, she would check in on me regularly. You're always watching over the rest of the crew. You need someone to watch over you, too, she'd said.

"Hey Massey, toss me one of those would you?" Hayes yelled and she threw a ration pack in his direction before heading over to talk to him.

"It's kind of weird, isn't it?" Ledoux said.

"What?" Hayes asked.

"Well, to us, it feels like we left Earth just yesterday. Back home, though, all our family and friends are ten years older."

Ten years may not make a huge difference in the big scheme of things, but the twenty years plus that will have passed by the time we got home surely would. We, on the other hand, would remain basically the same thanks to the cryo-tech that enabled us to make this trip. The point of cryo-chambers was not to keep us young, necessarily. It had mostly to do with keeping our load, and thus the weight of the ship, as low as possible. It meant twenty years less of food and supplies that we needed to keep us alive. Plus, in the cryo room, there was extra protection from solar rays and any other dangerous radiation or contaminants we might come across. The hardly aging thing was just an added benefit.

"Kind of feels like a hundred years have passed to me," Massey said, rolling her shoulders and tipping her head to stretch her neck.

"That's just the cryo-fatigue," I said. "The muscle tightness and weakness will wear off soon. In the meantime, we should all do some cardio and flexibility exercises to ease the symptoms."

"Hey, you stole my lines," Massey quipped. "How about you stick to your disciplines and I'll stick to mine?"

I couldn't help but smile at her. This was a bit of a running joke between us. Medicine and physiology often overlapped, so there'd been a few teasing arguments about who should deal with what.

"Yeah, we'll get right on that exercise thing," Hayes said, "after we eat and check the data."

We were all scientists on the mission of the century. We were the first live crew to make it this far into space. As much as I tried to play the cool-headed, reasonable one, I had to admit that I was just as excited as everyone else.

We finished our meal of rations quickly after that. Soon each of us was seated in front of holographic computer terminals with 3D images, poring over the ten years of data that had collected while we slept.

It seemed like barely a moment had passed when Boyton said, "We're here, ladies and gentlemen." We all headed over to the view-screen, which was about six times as large as the window in the mess hall, thankfully. If it hadn't been, there would likely be five adult scientists fighting like school kids to be first to see the incredible view.

There ahead of us was Neptune in all its bright-blue glory. To our left was one of its fourteen moons. The planet was an awe-inspiring sight, its color so much more vibrant than photos taken by probes had any chance to do justice.

Once we reached the capture point that would pull us into orbit around the mysterious planet, we would quickly lose visual on it. Soon after that, we'd move into the powerful magnetic field that flowed out behind it, and we'd lose most of our exterior sensors as well. With the limited windows of time we had to observe the planet with our own eyes, I wanted to just stand there and soak it all in.

I'm not sure how long I stayed there, mouth agape, before I was finally able to shake myself free of the view and get back to work.

Two

The Mission

DAVON

Time on the Explorer 2 was measured by a clock that was set to match that of the World Aeronautics and Space Administration, or WASA, so that we were always synced with Mission Control. But the lack of a rising and setting sun—that we could see, anyway—messed with our sleep patterns a little. Most nights, we stayed up analyzing data until our eyes burned and arose again after only a short sleep. We were only going to be here for a limited amount of time, and I think we all wanted to take advantage of as much of it as possible.

Boyton and Hayes were scheduled to take turns sleeping so that one of them was always available to command and pilot the ship. That was strictly a 'just-in-case' thing since our route had been planned and plotted for us long before we embarked on this mission. The rest of us decided we would stick to the same schedule for now, since we wanted to compare notes on the data.

The day we were expecting to enter orbit around Neptune, Massey managed to talk us—all except Boyton—into doing yoga with her before we started for the day, and she led us through some poses. It was smart thinking on her part. We were all wound up and excited for this next part of our mission. There was a certain amount of uncertainty as well since we'd lose most of our sensors while our orbit took us around the back side of the gas giant. The yoga helped us work out some tension, stretch our muscles, and relax.

Once the yoga session ended, we chatted for a few moments about the day's plans before the women headed out to shower and change. I stayed behind with the intention to make use of some of the lightweight exercise equipment. I had my back to the door and jumped a little when I heard a voice from just behind me.

"Hey, Davon." It irritated me a little that Hayes took the liberty to use my first name. He was the only one who did so regularly, though he usually saved it for when we were alone or when he intended to flirt. So when I heard it, it tended to set me on guard.

I slowly turned towards him. "Hayes. What can I do for you?"

"Well, Doc, I have this pain in my groin. I'm afraid I might have strained something doing that pose. What was it called again?"

I tipped my head to the side and squinted at him. He had a smirk on his lips and looked to be in no more pain than my yoga mat was. "It's only been a few days, Hayes. Are you feeling that desperate already?"

"Come on, Davon. You know it's not like that for me."

I did know, though I tried to pretend I didn't. He'd been flirting with me regularly ever since he'd caught me drooling over a photo in a men's fitness magazine and he'd realized I wasn't straight. I still wondered, though, if he would be this interested if he hadn't known we'd be stuck together with few other options for a couple of decades. Not that it felt like decades, but still.

He was a good-looking man—handsome with a lean, muscular physique—but I didn't feel any spark with him. I'd turned down relationships with men I'd shared more attraction with in favor of this mission, and I wasn't about to let my body's physical needs lead me in this either. This was my life's work. It was too important to take chances with.

"I don't think it would be a good idea," I said. "We work together, in close proximity to each other and the rest of the crew."

"No one will care. We're adults, we can keep it professional the rest of the time. Really, what's a little frot between friends?"

I could feel the tightness around my eyes and mouth when I glared at him. He must have correctly read my expression because he lifted his hands in surrender and took a step back.

"Fine," he said. "I'll leave. But if you change your mind, you know where I live." He shot me a flirty smile and a wink before he turned around and walked out of the room.

To say I knew where he lived was an understatement, considering there were two shared bunkrooms on board, and he and Boyton shared mine. At least we had a folding door we could pull out to extend over the outside of our bunks, giving us a modicum of privacy. I would have to keep mine closed whenever I found myself alone in the room with Hayes.

I shook my head and went to grab a drink and some rations from the mess before heading to the showers. I wanted to give him time to finish in there before I took my turn.

Later that afternoon, we were all back in the main control room sitting at our terminals, oohing and ahhing over the readings our probes and sensors were collecting at this very moment as it descended into Neptune's upper layers. It had been more than a century and a half since the Voyager 2 had visited the planet; changes in technology allowed us to build equipment that was much more temperature and pressure resistant. We were all crossing our fingers that it was enough, and that the probe would hold together long enough to get definite and detailed information about the core of the gas giant.

We were also going to be dropping probes to thirteen of Neptune's moons. But for the fourteenth, Triton—the only moon that orbited in retrograde—we would be taking a lander down there for a personal visit. Scientists had been working on creating suits to withstand the cold temperatures for more than sixty years before they had the breakthrough that would allow us to go down there, and I was among the lucky crew that would be the first to set foot on Triton's frozen surface. These were amazing times we were in, and I could not wait to get down there.

We were nearing the capture point and would lose our external sensors soon, so we were gathering as much information as we could before that happened. We'd be able to get more data once we moved far enough around the planet that we were past the magnetic field, but it kind of felt like we were kids being handed a birthday present that we could only unwrap partway before having to set it aside and wait until the next day to finish. What kid had the patience and self-control for that? We would send down another probe on the other side of the planet once we were there.

Boyton and Ledoux were now sitting at their control stations, getting ready for the maneuvers to come. The navigational computers had been preloaded with everything they needed to get us through our mission, but Captain Boyton and Ledoux still needed to run the math in case of any errors or any changes that may have occurred in the ten years we'd been traveling.

"Retrograde engines firing," Ledoux said, just before there was a slight lurch. A short time later, she announced, "Arriving at capture point." That was all that signaled that we were now being pulled around in orbit of the planet by its gravitational field, since our trajectory and speed had been programed to match it.

I sat in my seat in the control room, watching them and the monitors with awe. We were now in orbit of Neptune. I kept my eye open for a dark spot on the surface, wondering where it might have moved to, or even if there still was one. There had been much speculation about it before images from the Voyager 2 proved that it had been a massive storm system that then disappeared in the next image sets, only to reappear in a different area.

"Approaching the magnetic wake," Ledoux announced. "We'll be losing visuals and external sensors in two minutes."

"Roger that," Boyton said.

"Switching to LiDAR," said Ledoux.

"Pax, eyes on," Boyton said. I made my way over to the set-up that was somewhere between binoculars and a telescope that allowed us to see what lay in our path when the sensors were out.

The reality of space was much different than the sci-fi horror movies Hayes liked to watch. It was vast, there was no up and down, and at any point there were countless different directions you could look in. What you were looking for could be right there in your sight range, but you could still overlook it in the vastness of the universe. Luckily for me, we just needed to look ahead to ensure that nothing had moved into our path in the years between the initial calculations and now.

We worked in silence for a while, Boyton making sure all the calculations were as they should be, Ledoux keeping an eye on the LiDAR images and me keeping an eye out through one of the few ways we could physically see outside, just in case the LiDAR missed anything. Redundant? Maybe. But the stakes were high out here.

"Captain Boyton," I heard Ledoux say, "there's something here at the edge of this LiDAR image. None of our surveillance from Earth suggested we'd find anything in that area."

"Could it be an error?"

"That's what I thought at first, but it's on three different images, then it disappears as our nose comes around."

"Can you tell what it is?" Hayes asked.

"No, the images aren't clear enough. This could be something new. Maybe another object that's being captured by Neptune? It's possible we missed it from Earth and the Voyagers because of where it's located. Can we stop to investigate?"

Captain Boyton was quiet for a moment before answering. "I think that until we have extra fuel safely on board, we should be careful with what we have. We'll continue on with the mission as planned."

"But Captain—"

He raised a hand to stay her response. "Once we're safely in orbit around Triton we'll set up some equipment and point it in the right direction in the hopes of seeing what it is. And once we have more fuel on board, we should be good to take another orbit around Neptune if we haven't figured it out by then."

"Yes sir," Ledoux said.

I could tell from her voice that she was disappointed and I could understand where she was coming from. An astronomer slash cosmologist slash astrophysicist out here orbiting Neptune finds possible evidence of a previously unknown body in our solar system, of course she'd be excited. But I understood where Boyton was coming from as well. He had the entire crew's lives and the mission's success to think about.

Three

Unexpected

DAVON

When we were through the magnetic field, we started the orbital transfer to switch from our current orbital plane to Neptune's orbital plane. Inclination changes took a lot of energy, but the point in coming out here was to study Neptune and Triton, and that was best done from Neptune's plane. This was one of the reasons why we needed to collect fuel from Neptune's atmosphere. If we got enough, we'd gain more time to stay and study the planet and it's one moon that moved as no other moon in our solar system did.

Once we were in the correct plane, we sent out another probe so we'd have readings from the opposite side of the planet from the first probe. As we approached Triton, we passed to its left, allowing the ship to be captured in its orbit, where we would stay for a while as our probes gathered information from

Neptune. We would use probes for Triton as well, but with our gear it would be safe to go down there in the lander as well, to investigate in person. I would be among the first to ever set foot on Triton, and it still blew my mind that I was lucky enough to get this honor.

Now that our sensors and cameras were back on line, Ledoux pointed a few in the direction of the anomaly she had seen on the LiDAR images. I looked over her shoulder at them.

"Do you think the object is in orbit as well?" I asked.

"I do," she said.

"Just look here, Pax." She pointed to the images. "The images were taken one right after the other, so it's hard to tell. Do you think it moved at all?"

I squinted down at the spots she pointed out. "I'm not sure. Is there a fixed point to measure against?"

She had just opened her mouth to answer when a beeping started to sound at regular intervals. Ledoux jumped up from the images and ran over to the bank of a dozen monitors, each one showing a different image from a sensor or camera. Now, I may have been a doctor slash microbiologist, but I was also a science nerd who'd been obsessed with space almost my entire life. So I followed her, of course.

"What is it?" I asked. She turned and grabbed my shoulders and shook them a little. "It was in orbit! It's moving closer to us now."

"That's so exciting! When do we get to see what it is?"

"In just a minute. I have to adjust one of the cameras."

As she fiddled with the controls, I watched the screen and, suddenly, there it was. The speed at which it arrived surprised me, especially given that movement could barely be seen on the LiDAR images, suggesting it had been moving slowly.

From this angle, it looked like a smooth, black object that was surprisingly uniform. As I watched, I realized it was somewhat in the shape of a teardrop, if it were laying on its side. "Is it normal for an object in space to be that smooth?"

By now, the others had gathered around, standing behind her chair, as I was.

"Not really normal from what we've seen to date," she said. "But who knows? No one but us has ever been out this far in space before."

"What's that?" Massey pointed at the screen as we continued to watch.

At first, I didn't see what she was talking about. But then, I noticed it.

"Am I seeing what I think I'm seeing?" Hayes chimed in.

"That depends," I answered. "Do you see a red glow in the front that seems to be growing brighter by the second?"

"Shit!" Hayes said, loud enough that I startled and looked at him. His eyes were wide. "That's a fucking space ship! And I think it's going to fire on us."

"Don't be ridicul..."

Ledoux didn't get to finish her sentence before a round opening formed in the front of the object.

"I think Hayes is right." I said.

But it didn't matter. If it was a ship preparing to fire on us, it would be too late for us to do anything about it. We were a scientific research vessel that had expected to find nothing but inanimate objects to study. We had no means of retaliating, or even protecting ourselves.

It seemed kind of ironic that the proof there was other intelligent life out here would be the very last thing we would ever see. We wouldn't even have time to let anyone else know.

Just as the alien craft fired on us, however, it was hit by something that sent it spinning and sent its shot slightly off target. We heard the sound of metal rending followed quickly by alarms going off.

"Hang on!" I heard Boyton shout. The ship lurched and a glance at the window showed we were moving.

Hayes was now manning the co-pilot controls and he and Boyton were shouting things back and forth to each other. I just sat myself in a seat and held on, just in case.

In what seemed to be both an eternity and a blink of an eye, Boyton yelled, "We're back in orbit."

I hadn't even realized we'd been out of orbit. I looked at Ledoux, who'd been white knuckling the console as she watched the monitors.

"What happened?" I asked.

"First of all, Ledoux," Boyton said, "are we out of danger?"

Ledoux worked the controls and looked at the monitors. "Looks like the danger is over, at least for now."

I breathed a sigh of relief, until she added, "Who knows what else might be hiding out there."

"Agreed," Boyton said. "Keep alert, everyone."

"So, what happened?" Hayes said, repeating my earlier question.

By now, Massey had made her way over to us as well, and we all watched as Ledoux played videos of the scene from a couple of different angles. No one said a word as we witnessed the alien vessel fire on us at the same time as it was hit by a shot from a second vessel that looked exactly like the first. That sent the first vessel spinning, but it quickly recovered and took aim at the second ship, which was heading in our direction. The second ship received a direct hit but managed to get another one in on the first.

At the end, the first vessel—the one that had fired on us—was sent drifting off into space. In the direction it was heading it would probably be floating for some time before it encountered anything, unless it could get itself back on line again. In which case, I assumed we'd better be prepared to be attacked again.

The second vessel—the one that seemed to have saved us—tried to stabilize itself before it lost power. It was now slowly floating in the direction of Triton.

I heard Hayes give a long, low whistle. "How the hell were those ships moving like that out here?"

"They obviously have better tech than we do," Boyton said.

"Are we out of danger?" Massey asked. "We were hit, weren't we?"

Boyton headed back to his computer terminal and checked out the ship's systems. "We have a gouge in our outer hull," he said. "Front portside. Also, it looks like our long-distance communications array is damaged. We won't be able to contact Earth until it's fixed, and that won't happen until someone gets out there to fix it."

"On it," Hayes said, and he headed off in the direction of engineering and the supply bay.

"So, what do we do now?" Massey asked.

"We do what we came here to do," Boyton said. "You all may need to help out in areas you weren't expecting with Hayes heading outside, but we still need to launch the skimmer to collect fuel, and we'll send a probe towards Triton to see if it's safe to go down there to collect samples."

"That other ship that's headed for Triton, what do we do about that?" I asked.

"Well, Pax, I think that might be a perfect opportunity for our medical officer and biologist to be the first person to find definitive proof of intelligent life beyond our own."

Boyton, Hayes, Ledoux, Massey and I all gathered close to the monitor as the Captain adjusted one of our exterior cameras to focus on the object that had crash-landed, almost in slow-motion, on Triton.

Hayes had already been outside and came back stating that the array was pretty much toast, and we didn't have what we needed to fix it. He might be able to jerry-rig something from what we had, he'd told us, but then Boyton decided he needed to be with the rest of the crew as we tried to figure out what to do next.

From just a superficial viewing, the alien vessel could have been mistaken for an oblong-shaped rock made smooth on its journeys, but there were a few uniformly shaped areas that seemed more smooth than the surfaces surrounding them. It immediately brought to mind those vehicles back on Earth that were all one color with windows tinted the same shade. They would look like one solid object if not for the seams of the doors.

"Are there any cracks along the surface?" I asked.

Boyton was quiet for a moment as he panned the camera around. "I can't be sure from here. We might need to get a closer look. Maybe send a probe down there."

"We could probably get samples from it if we go down there instead of sending a probe," Hayes suggested. "Maybe Pax could go down there with one of his biology kits. We might even be able to check out the tech."

"Me?" I squeaked. After looking forward to a chance like this for years, I now found myself feeling nervous. Maybe it was because there was now intelligent alien life involved. Given I was a doctor and biologist, this should have excited me. However, I suddenly found scenes from the alien horror films Hayes made me watch flickering through my mind. After the first two, I caught on to the subject matter and refused to watch any more of them, but what had been seen could not be unseen.

"Well, you're the micro-biologist, aren't you?" Hayes said. "Why wouldn't you be excited to go down there? I mean, didn't you come on this mission in the hopes of discovering life?"

"I blame my nerves on you, Hayes, because of those movies you tricked me into watching."

"That's why I'm going with you, Pax," Hayes said, slapping his hand down on my shoulder and giving it a squeeze.

"Pax," Captain Boyton added, "if there is a living—or previously living—being in that thing...well, just think about it. You could be the very first human to discover proof of intelligent life other than our own."

I took in his words. He was right of course. That would be huge.

"Whoever or whatever is in that thing," Massey added, "just risked their life to save us."

"Unless that was a coincidence," Hayes mumbled from next to me. Massey shot him a dark look.

"I doubt very much that an intelligent life form would do such a thing if they meant us harm," Massey continued.

"Unless they were fighting with that other ship and we just happened to be here."

"Shut it, Hayes!" Ledoux barked.

"What? I'm just playing," he said, feigning innocence. "You know I'm just playing, right Pax?"

"Sure," I said. "And that's why I'm going to let you approach the alien ship first."

"That's assuming there's even anything in there," Boyton said. "It could be controlled remotely for all we know, like our probes."

"That would be even more awesome tech to explore," Hayes said. "Imagine, though, if we could figure out how they maneuvered like they did, and how they traveled so quickly. Think of how the future of space travel would be changed if we could learn that and apply it to our own space vessels."

I nodded absently at the conversation as I continued to look at the images of the ship on Triton. But it was Massey's words that repeated in my head right now. She was right. If there were intelligent beings in that craft, they just risked their lives to save us. They could be down there, severely injured and dying, while I was up here fighting irrational, fiction-based fears.

Shit. What kind of a doctor was I?

I nodded resolutely. "Alright. Let's do this, Hayes."

He grinned widely. "Now you're talking."

Four

Guest

DAVON

The lander descended slowly onto the surface of Triton. We'd sent a probe out ahead of us just to ensure there were no dangers that couldn't be seen from our ship's cameras. We'd found nothing that our suits couldn't handle. Still, since we weren't sure what we'd find, Massey, who was also trained to act as my medical assistant when need be, was back on the ship putting the quarantine protocols into place in the medical bay, just in case.

"You know, in one movie—I think this one might have been my favorite—when the soldiers went into the alien spacecraft—"

"Shut the fuck up with that shit, Hayes. Seriously, keep your mouth shut or I'll shut it for you." The man really knew how to push my buttons, and not in the way he seemed to hope. The only times I swore like this were around him.

"Hey, don't worry, I'll protect you, Davon."

Shit. Was that his game? I glared at him.

"I can protect myself, thank you very much."

"Look," he continued, gesturing to his belt. "I even have my laser rock-cutter. I'm sure whatever is in there isn't any tougher than space rock."

My eyes widened. Now I was worried for an entirely different reason.

"Goddammit, Hayes. Remember what I said: No starting any wars because you assumed the worse first."

He lifted his hands in the air in a gesture of innocence.

I shook my head. "Why do you always have to be such a pain in my ass?"

"Well, I haven't been yet, not for lack of trying," he said in a salacious tone. "Don't worry though, I promise you'd enjoy it."

"Really?" I asked, giving him my best glare. "You really think this is the right time for this crap?"

"Is there ever really a wrong time, Davon?" He raised an eyebrow at me flirtatiously.

The man was seriously playing with fire. I was already on edge, and he was annoying the hell out of me. If we'd been back on Earth, I'd be about ready to contact HR and report him for harassment. Luckily for him, the comm started giving the alert that we were approaching the landing site. If I hadn't intended to make him go first, I would have probably laid him out cold and left him there in a heap.

"Shut up and put your helmet on, Hayes."

He gave me a sarcastic salute—yes, salutes can be sarcastic, and Hayes was the master of them—and put his helmet on. Then we were silent, thankfully, as we landed. We descended the ladder into the lower compartment, closing the upper door before opening the airlock and making our way the rest of the way down, onto the surface of Triton itself.

I was below Hayes, so it was my foot that touched the rocky surface first. At that point, my nerves disappeared and all that was left was wonder. I was the very first human to set foot on Triton. I took a deep breath, my heart pounding; I suddenly felt overwhelmed with some feeling I could not quite name. This moment was one for the history books.

As a child, my dream was to be among the first to see the outer planets through the window of a spaceship. That dream had just been blown out of the solar system. I looked up from the ground to spot the alien vessel perhaps twenty meters ahead, and I realized I may soon be the first human to have contact with an alien race.

Yes, the dream had been blown away numerous times over. What in the universe had I been nervous about? We were making history here.

Without waiting for word from Hayes, I made my way forward toward the ship. A visit to Triton was on our mission list, so we'd fortunately practiced in a low-gravity chamber that had been made to represent a gravity of 8 percent of Earth's. I needed to exert very little effort to move and pushing off from the surface with too much force would send us floating in the air only to slowly fall back again. It sounded like fun, actually, but not when there was potentially a life on the line, so I kept my movements soft and careful.

I heard my own breathing echo inside my helmet, and I could hear Hayes's through the comm device. I smiled when I realized it was Hayes's breathing that picked up speed and hitched now and then as we got closer, not my own.

When we arrived at the ship, Hayes said, "I don't see any doors or openings of any kind. I'm going to try the rock laser."

"Just hold on. This ship survived being shot at and crash-landing here with only a few dents. Well, a couple of good dents, sure, but you know what I mean. Let's examine it to see if we can find any way to open it before we waste fuel trying to cut through it."

Hayes gave a put-upon sigh, like I was depriving him of playing with a toy. "Fine. Let's both start at the front here and we can each take a side and meet at the back."

"Sounds good," I said. "And remember, Hayes, to work very carefully. Trip and fall against this thing and we'll be chasing after it."

I had no idea how much a spaceship like this one weighed, of course. Probably a couple of tons. However, since I also didn't know what kind of materials it was made from, that was purely a guess, not a scientific hypothesis.

Reaching out my gloved hand, I gently ran it along the surface while slowly making my way toward the back. Since our gloves were thick and bulky, I also made sure to give the surface a careful visual inspection as I went. I had just noticed an uneven bump in the surface when I heard Hayes over the comm.

"Uh, Doc. You might want to come over here."

I quickly made my way to the other side of the alien spacecraft, then stopped in my tracks. There was a side door that I assumed slid open, though I couldn't see where it had gone.

"How did you get it open?" I asked.

Hayes shook his head. "I have no idea. I mean, it might have been me, but I'm thinking that, chances are, it was that guy." He gestured to the open side of the ship.

I slowly took a couple of more steps toward the door until I saw what he was pointing at. Then, my eyes glued to the form in front of me. It was all black, with no visible eyes or other facial features, though its other physical characteristics were very similar to that of a human male—one who was approximately seven feet tall with wide shoulders and a muscular torso.

"This is weird shit, Doc. This thing doesn't even have a face."

I moved closer still. "Hello? Can you hear me?" There was no response. I tapped on the alien's shoulder and repeated my question. Then I leaned in carefully to inspect the creature more closely.

"Actually, Hayes, I think he's wearing a suit."

"A suit?"

"Yes. You know, like the ones you and I are wearing to protect us from the dangers of space. Only his is a little more form-fitting."

"Maybe we should get the name of his tailor."

Hayes's words were joking, but his voice shook and cracked a little.

"Do you think it's alive?" he asked.

"I'm not sure." I cursed the thickness of my gloves. Checking vitals by hand would be impossible. I pulled my scanner from my belt. "I don't know if this scanner will pick up anything, or even what I should be looking for."

"Well, he looks humanoid."

"Doesn't mean everything will be the same on the inside." I was now leaning partly over the alien's torso, trying to pick up any readings. So I jumped when his head shifted slightly in my direction. I sucked in a breath, thinking he had woken up and not knowing how he would react finding an alien in his personal space. If it were me, I'd probably have a panic attack. So I stood there, stock still and waiting, for a couple of minutes. When there was no further movement, I let out a sigh of relief. He wasn't dead, and he wasn't a threat. At least for now.

"We need to get him up to the Explorer 2," I said. "It looks like the opposite side of the vessel is crushed up against his side. We're going to have to pry him out. Very carefully."

"Are you sure it's okay to bring it on board?" the space horror-film aficionado asked. "Maybe we should leave it here until we figure out if it's safe."

I looked over my shoulder at Hayes, who was standing close, watching what I was doing.

"I'm not about to let him stay here and die when he's in this situation because he saved our lives."

"Fine, but if it ends up eating us all, or infecting us with some alien virus, that's on you."

"I'll make sure to document everything and send notes back to Earth every couple of hours once the long-distance array is back up. That way if we die, they'll at least have a record of what happened."

"Yeah, sure. That's a great comfort. Thanks." His tone was dry and flat.

I chuckled. "You really need to stop watching those horror movies, Hayes."

He mumbled something that sounded suspiciously like, "I'm not scared, you're scared," before moving forward to help me.

It took some maneuvering, especially in our bulky suits, but we finally got the alien out and loaded on the lander—a task made both easier and harder by the low gravity—and we were soon on our way back to the Explorer 2.

꘎ ♥ ꘎ ♥ ꘎

Once Hayes and I were back on board the lander with our new guest secured, we contacted the Explorer 2 to let them know to double check that the medical bay was secured according to the strictest quarantine protocols. The room would be completely sealed—not just against contaminants, but also to prevent the escape of patients should symptoms lead to aggression or hallucinations. This was necessary since we would be in outer space with no options if the worse should happen.

When the lead engineers had first gone over this information with me, back when the Explorer 2 was under construction, I had laughed, thinking it was overkill. Now, however, I was grateful. I knew that chances were very slim that Captain Boyton would have agreed to bring an unknown alien onto our ship if we hadn't had such precautions in place.

Once back at the ship, Massey and Hayes helped me get the alien, who now felt much heavier, into the medical bay and onto a patient bed. The crew watched me as I hooked up and turned on equipment that, with any luck, would soon be giving me readings to help me figure out the physiology of my newest patient.

As I worked, I heard shuffling feet, whispered yet urgent conversation, and the crinkling of protective suits behind me. It was loud enough that I found it distracting. Especially since the comm devices that were built into the helmets of our protective suits meant I could hear them clearly, even though they thought they were keeping their voices down.

"You know," I said, "you two can wait outside if you're worried about the alien. I mean, you can see everything in here through the windows to the rest of the medical bay." We were currently in one of three secure treatment rooms.

"It's not that we're worried," Massey began. "Scratch that. It's not that I'm worried. Hayes here, on the other hand, thinks we should have left him out there on Triton."

I looked at Hayes, brows raised. He shrugged nonchalantly.

"We have no idea of its capabilities or its agenda," he said.

"And again, why would he have risked himself for us if he intended to harm us right afterward?"

Sylas shrugged again. "The thrill of the hunt?" he suggested.

I shook my head and returned to what I was doing. "If you're not comfortable, you can step out to the main room."

"And leave you in here with it alone? Not a chance."

"He's unconscious and strapped down. Nothing is going to happen."

That old saying 'famous last words' jumped into my head in the very next second. That was the moment the alien chose to jolt awake, tugging against the straps and gasping. Well, at least I assume that sound was gasping. I hadn't figured out how to get his suit open yet, so I couldn't see what was going on.

"Hey, hey, you're okay, you're okay," I said in soothing tones. I stepped toward him and he turned his head in my direction. It would have been useful in this moment if his suit had a visor like ours—not that I'm an expert at alien facial expressions. So, it probably wouldn't actually help, now that I thought about it.

He continued to pull at the restraints and began to speak in a language I couldn't understand. I wasn't an expert in alien vocal tones either, but if I were to guess, I would say he was becoming more agitated, and I didn't know what to do to help. But then I got an idea.

"Hayes, Massey. Step out of the room."

"What?" Hayes demanded. "Are you kidding me?"

"No, I'm not," I replied. "The readings in here say the air is clear, so I'm going to take off my helmet. I'm hoping he'll do the same, and since we don't know what's going on in there," I said, gesturing at the alien's suit, "I would rather be the only person put at risk."

"No way," Hayes said.

The alien was still speaking excitedly and was now leaning as far toward me as the restraints would allow. His body language didn't seem threatening, from what I could tell. Rather, it was as if he was trying to communicate something of great importance.

"It isn't your choice Hayes, it's mine as his doctor. Step out now or I'll be forced to get Boyton involved."

Hayes's lips pressed together and his eyes went stony behind his visor, but I couldn't focus on that. I needed to focus on my patient and figure out what he was trying to tell me. That was not going to be an easy task.

"Fine," Hayes bit out. "But we'll be right out there," he said, jabbing a finger towards the window. "If anything suspicious happens—"

"Yes, yes. I'll be sure to let you know and have you come rescue me."

Five

Acquaintance

DAVON

I watched Massey and Hayes leave the room and suddenly I felt as alone as I'd just declared, like an idiot, I wanted to be. I turned to look at the alien, and his voice gentled. He seemed to stare at me expectantly, but I couldn't be sure since I couldn't see his face.

I looked at the display on my forearm one more time to check for any changes in the air and, when I found none, I reached up to the releases on my helmet and started unfastening it from my suit. When I removed it, the patient stilled. I wasn't sure what that meant, but I was hit with the strong desire to see his face as well. To see how different we were.

My fingers trembled as I moved my hands to his restraints. He seemed to understand, since he allowed me close enough to do it. Then he sat still as I removed them.

The alien looked at me for a moment then reached up to his neck. I didn't see any buttons or anything, but whatever he did caused a display of some kind to light up the face of his suit. I didn't recognize any of the characters that popped up, of course, but I assumed he was doing the same thing I'd just done and checking to see if it was safe.

My assumption was confirmed when, a moment later, he traced a pattern on the helmet—or hood, whatever you could call it—of his suit; his index finger moved down from behind his ear, past his jawline, then down to where neck met shoulder. Then he drew his finger backwards. As he did so, the helmet split in the center and drew back and down until it disappeared into the body of his suit.

My eyes had been drawn to the movement but, once it was done, I looked at his face and sucked in a sharp breath.

The features before me were very human-like, the differences limited to color and the sharpness of the features. My patient's skin was a shade of light blue-gray, and his hair looked to be somewhere between a dark blue and purple; that didn't quite describe the color, but it was as close as I could get. His eyes were dark, probably black, and his facial features were sharp and defined.

On his neck just below his ear, there was a pattern of light brown spots, if you could call them that. They were irregularly shaped and went from a thin line near the top to a thicker line, made up of more and larger spots, where it disappeared into his suit. I took a couple of slow steps to the right and saw that the same type of pattern traveled down the other side of his neck as well. If I had seen those marks on a human, I would have assumed they were tattoos.

My eyes flickered up to his face again. This might not be a word commonly used to describe a male, but he was beautiful.

I think I must have just stood there staring for some time before he tilted his head and started speaking in that foreign language again. I would have been embarrassed to have been caught drooling over him like I'd been, but his voice became urgent again, even though it stayed soft, and I decided I needed to make trying to communicate the priority at that moment.

I held up a finger to signal to him to wait a moment, then immediately hoped that wasn't a rude gesture where he was from. I hurried to the desk at the other side of the room and grabbed my medical tablet, then returned to my spot near the foot of his bed. Placing my hand on my chest, I said, "I'm Davon Pax." I patted my chest again and said, "Davon."

I couldn't help but smile wide when he repeated my name perfectly. I nodded and asked, "What's your name?" I pointed to him. He placed his hand against his own chest and said, "Tulq'on."

I internally sighed with relief at the fact that his name seemed pronounceable in English.

"Til-con?" I repeated. He shook his head and said it again, this time more slowly, articulating each syllable.

"Tulq-on."

"Tulq'on," I repeated, pretty sure I had gotten it right this time. Thankfully, he nodded.

"Tulq'on, I'm a doctor." I repeated the word, "doctor," then I brought up images on my medical tablet in the hopes of teaching him what I meant. I showed him pictures of doctors studying human anatomy, doctors treating patients, and doctors operating on injuries too severe for superficial treatments. Then I repeated "doctor" once again and placed my hand on my chest.

I was more pleased than I had any right to be when he easily repeated the word. I went on to explain, using words, gestures, and a drawing app on my tablet, that his ship had crashed and I wanted to check him for injuries. I had scanned him and found, as expected, that his heartbeat, blood pressure and temperature were all slightly different than a human's. Since I had no baseline, I was just monitoring them for any changes. Scanners could show me inside his body as well, but since I didn't know what was normal for his species, I wanted to check him over by hand to see if there were any external areas that looked different from the rest of him, assuming they could be injuries.

I removed the rest of my space suit, leaving myself in the undergarments that covered us from wrist to ankles underneath, then I gestured for him to do the same. Luckily, he understood. I think it would be fair to use the term "peeled off" to describe him getting out of his suit, since it was so form-fitting.

When Tulq'on stood to pull the suit down over his legs, I had to crane my neck back to look at him, even from about two feet away. I was 5'11" and I would guess he was at least seven feet.

My eyes dragged down over his form. His shoulders were broad and roped with muscle, as were his chest and arms. His height and obvious strength should have left me feeling anxious and intimidated. Instead, I felt...ah hem, something decidedly not those things.

Once his suit was off I gestured to his underclothing. Though tight, they covered a large portion of his body and needed to come off as well if I were going to examine him properly. I opened a blanket, held it out in front of me, and turned my head to the side to give him some privacy. When nothing seemed to be happening, I glanced back to see him looking at me curiously, so I mimed taking off my clothes and held the blanket up again. I heard the swooshing sounds of clothes coming off, then felt cool hands over mine as he took the blanket from me.

My skin tingled where he touched me, but that was not the sensation that caused me to suck in a sharp breath and jerk my head around to look at him.

Tulq'on looked back at me with his head tilted and brows drawn down as he obviously considered me. Then he smiled wide, seemingly pleased, as he sat back on the bed.

When he'd touched me I'd been flooded with emotions: concern, worry, anxiety, urgency. These were not emotions I'd been feeling in that moment, I was sure. I continued to stare at him in wonder as I realized they'd been his feelings.

It felt almost ridiculous to think it, since such a thing only existed in films and books back on Earth. But this was not Earth, and he was not human. I might not have known yet what his species was called, but I did know one thing for certain: Tulq'on was an empath.

Then I was hit with an embarrassing thought: had he felt my emotions in that moment? Shit!

"Priorities, Davon, priorities," I mumbled to myself.

My embarrassment was not a priority. Making sure my patient wasn't suffering from internal injuries, then finding a way to communicate were. There was obviously something he was concerned about that he wanted to share with me. I had to figure out a way to make that happen.

I cleared my throat and got to work checking him over head to toe. Since he'd been in a crash, I did not want to skip anything and end up missing something potentially lethal. I'd seen that happen before when I did rounds in an emergency room as a resident and I did not want that to happen under my care.

His tattoo-like pattern traveled down until the two sides joined over his sternum before flaring out again and disappearing under the small of his back. My fingers wanted to follow them like a trail instead of the usual quick survey I was used to making. I managed to keep myself in professional mode and focus on what I was doing. I was extremely interested in learning more about this beautiful, alien creature, both as a doctor and scientist, and as myself.

When I got to his ribs I saw his left side was discolored and bruised. I started with palpating his apparently good side, needing to have something to compare the injured side to. He jerked a little and sucked in a breath when I checked out the bruised area. I was fairly certain that there was no fracture, though, just a large tender area. I also discovered that he had one more rib on each side than humans.

I kept checking down over his hips and along each leg, all the way down to his feet. At the outside of each hip, his tattoo-like spots flared out again, with one narrow line going down the front of each leg. When I checked out his back, I noticed that a line also went down the back of each leg. The design also split out again at the lower back and traveled upwards, joining then flaring out again. This time, the dotted pattern joined in the center at the base of his skull and disappeared underneath his hair. Once I was done, I motioned for him to turn onto his back again.

I looked up to speak to him, but my words got caught in my throat when I noticed the very large tent in the blanket that I'd been delicately adjusting over the center of his body as I'd worked. Apparently his anatomy was very much like that of a human male, and it had very much enjoyed my examination. I belatedly realized that I'd been lightly trailing my fingers along the path of his markings without conscious intentions to do so. I jerked my hand away from him and felt my face heat with embarrassment.

I tore my eyes away from...that and lifted my gaze to meet his. His stare was intense, seemingly impassive, yet his eyes moved back and forth across my face as if searching for something. I almost lost my breath just looking into those eyes, whose dark irises were larger than humans', making his eyes look blown-out.

"Um," I said, feeling a little, ahem, uncomfortable myself, "I'm just going to go grab something to apply to your ribs." I accompanied my words with gestures. I might have overexaggerated them a little.

I spun around and hurried to the supply cabinet. I took a few deep breaths to try and calm myself some, grabbed what I was looking for and turned to head back. My gaze snagged on the window, where I saw Hayes watching me with a thoughtful expression and Massey standing a few feet behind him. I felt my cheeks heat once again and I ducked my head, watching the floor until I got back to my patient.

Everything I'd seen up to now indicated that his anatomy was similar to ours, so I hoped this treatment would benefit him the same way it did humans. I unfolded the large bandage and laid it out over Tulq'on's injured ribs, pressing it to the area gently.

"These bandages are a marvel of human invention," I said. "They keep the area cool and release a substance to help numb the pain. It also should help speed up your recovery. Not that I know how long it normally takes you to heal." I knew he didn't understand me, but I always spoke to my patients, even if they were unconscious, so I did it without thinking. This time, however, my words were a little hurried and shaky.

"Davon."

My head jerked up and my eyes met his at the sound of my name on his lips. One large hand encircled my wrist and pulled me forward until he could place his other hand on my cheek. Then I felt it again—his emotions. I felt his fascination, his desire, and I wondered if he could feel mine too. His thumb stroked back and forth across my cheekbone and his eyes held mine ensnared.

"Davon," he said again, and he let out a sigh. I felt fondness, affection, and longing from him. Then he shook his head and I could sense the shift in his emotions. Again, I felt the worry and the anxiousness. I knew he had something he wanted to tell me. No, needed to tell me. He was frustrated at a lack of a way to communicate.

A knock at the window had me jerking back and turning. Hayes was beckoning me to come outside.

I turned back to Tulq'on. "I have to go for a few minutes," I said. "But I'll be back soon." Then I got an idea. I went to the cupboard above the desk and grabbed a tablet. I brought it back over to Tulq'on, opened the application I wanted and showed it to him.

"This is a language application," I said as I scrolled through and set it up. "You can choose any language on Earth. I'm going to set it to English, since that is what I usually speak. Luckily, it's set up as immersion learning, so it doesn't matter what language you're starting from." I brought up a page of words and images and hit the play button so he could hear the word sounded out. Tulq'on looked up and gave me a nod of understanding.

"Maybe you can go over this while I go check in out there." His focus was already on the tablet, so I turned and walked out to the open area of the medical bay.

Six

Communication

DAVON

W hat's going on in there?" Hayes questioned almost as soon as I'd walked through the door.

"Nothing!" I answered defensively, then remembered I didn't have to explain myself. I did, however, owe the crew an update on the situation.

"Hayes, can you call Captain Boyton and Ledoux here, please?"

He used the comm of his helmet to do as I asked. "You can take off the suits now," I said. "There's no indication of contaminants."

"Are you sure there are no alien germs that our tech can't pick up?"

"Well, if there were I wouldn't know, would I?" I snapped. Then I took a deep breath. "Sorry. I'm just tense." Probably the residual effects of feeling Tulq'on's frustration and anxiety. Of course, it could also be that there's an alien in my patient room—an alien that I was feeling inexplicably drawn to. "Just, go get out of your suits. There's a 99.8% chance that it's safe."

"Fine," Hayes said, "but if I get sick from alien germs and die, I'm going to come back to haunt you."

"Fair enough."

As they passed by me, Massey raised her eyebrows and gave me wide eyes, making me smile.

They were back within a few minutes, and Boyton and Ledoux arrived around the same time.

I caught them up about the alien's physical health, and then got to what I now believed was the more important part.

"His name is Tulq'on, and I'm sure he's worried about something. He's been trying to communicate with me." For some reason, I didn't want to tell them about him sharing his emotions with me. It seemed like it should be a private thing and he should be the one to choose with whom he shares that part of himself.

"Is that why he had his hands all over you?" Hayes asked.

My anger flared, but I instantly tamped it down. Hayes was acting like a possessive ass when he had absolutely no right to do so. But right now, I needed to focus on giving my theory to the others.

"Actually, I think he was trying to convey the urgency of the matter."

"And what matter is that?" Boyton asked.

"Well, that's the problem. I don't know. I need to find some way to communicate with him."

"Maybe it's about the ship that attacked us. Do you think there could be more headed our way? Or headed toward Earth?" Ledoux asked.

"Maybe. But until I can find out more, all we have are guesses."

"Why does it have to be you?" Hayes questioned. "Why can't someone else do it?"

"Well, we can't let you do it," Massey said. "You're likely to start an intergalactic war or something."

I dipped my chin down to hide my grin. Apparently I wasn't the only one Hayes was annoying. It's a good thing we were in cryo-sleep on the trip here and would be again on the way back.

I looked up at Boyton and addressed my comments to him. "I've already started to build a rapport with him, and I know the most languages of all of us. I can try to apply what I know and see if that gets us anywhere. Plus, let's face it, unless everyone starts getting sick or injured, I'm the least needed out there." I gestured to the control room. "I am also the medical doctor on board and a biologist, so obviously an injured alien would be more within my areas of expertise."

Boyton nodded. "Agreed. But you need to take care of yourself. Eat, sleep, all of that. So, we'll take turns guarding him whenever you're not here."

"With respect, Captain, I think whatever he's trying to tell me is important enough that I should try to figure it out as soon as possible. This is an alien here, one who just saved us from an unexplained attack. I have a feeling that the sooner we can figure this out, the better. I promise, though, if I get too tired or need a break, I'll let you know so someone can take over while I'm gone."

Boyton paused in thought for a moment before nodding his head in agreement. "Fine, but we'll leave the emergency security measures up around the med bay and you call one of us if anything comes up."

"Of course, Captain."

With that, the four other crew members left, and I turned to head back to my patient once again.

I glanced through the window before reentering the room. Tulq'on was absorbed in the tablet I'd given him. I tried to enter quietly so as not to disturb him, but his head jerked up as soon as I opened the door.

"Davon," he said, then he lifted the tablet in my direction and pointed to it. I went over to look at what he wanted to show me. It seemed he'd found the drawing application as well. He scooted over a little and I took the hint and sat down. I was immediately aware of his closeness to me. When he didn't say anything right away, I looked up to find him staring at me. My breath caught. The chemistry between us was intense—almost more than I could handle—and my gaze was trapped by his for a moment. As soon as I could tear my eyes away from him, I tapped the tablet and looked down again.

"Do you have something to show me?"

"Yes," he said. I jerked my head up in surprise. He smiled at my reaction but quickly refocused on the tablet.

He began to draw an image, and as I watched I could see the picture forming. There was the Kuiper belt; on this side of it, he drew Pluto, Neptune, Triton, and what looked to be The Explorer 2. On the outside of the belt, he drew a ship that was shaped like the one he'd arrived in. Then he drew another that looked about a tenth the size of the first out in the asteroid field.

Tulq'on flipped back to the language application and searched something in the dictionary. Then he returned to the image he had drawn.

"Co-man-duh sheep," he said, tapping his finger on the larger of the two vessels.

I thought for a moment about what he might mean. "Command ship?" I asked, and he nodded. He pointed at the image again, this time tapping the smaller vessel.

"Tulq'on," he said.

"That's your ship?" I asked to verify.

"Yes."

He continued drawing, this time showing lines from the command ship through the asteroid belt. Then the line continued at an angle until it met The Explorer 2, and near us he drew another vessel shaped like his own. I looked at him in shock when I realized what he was trying to explain.

"Are you saying the command ship purposely sent that ship to fire on us?" There was a grunt of agreement.

"But why?" I asked. I didn't expect him to understand but, to my surprise, he did, and he attempted to give me an answer.

"Co-mmand not like humans." He turned the virtual page to a clear one and continued drawing. After a few minutes, the picture started to become clearer.

There were no features on the little humanoid figures he sketched, but they stretched across the planet they were on. He filled in the solar system in the background as well, and it soon became obvious that the planet he was referring to was Earth, and all the little people he'd drawn on it were fighting each other and damaging the Earth. It may not have been an exact, historically accurate version of events, but I understood what he was telling me.

"We have not been like that for a long time. We've become so much better. There hasn't been war in over a century and a half. We try to be accepting and understanding of one another. There are always outliers, of course, but we do try. We've built a base on the moon with a space station and started numerous projects focused on the betterment of the Earth. All the time, money, and energy we used for war and prejudice before? We've been trying to focus them on learning, on building bridges, on exploring our universe." I made a sweeping gesture with my arm. "We are trying to fix our mistakes."

"Tulq'on know. I watch." He tapped his finger on the drawing of the Earth. "I... study."

It took me a moment to grasp what he was saying. I had no idea how he could have observed us without us noticing, but there was a lot I didn't know, apparently.

"Is that how you've learned so much English so quickly? You didn't learn it all just now, did you?"

"Um," he said. It was a sound of agreement. "Also..." He went back to the tablet, clearing the virtual page and drawing again.

I watched as the image took shape. He drew from a bird's eye-view at first, showing a ten sided-polygon with a circle ringing it. Then he drew another image next to it. Soon, I could understand that he was showing the polygon from the side, and the circle now looked conical from this angle. Then he drew what looked to be a boom with a three-sectioned cylinder on the end. On the opposite side he added another boom. This time some attached sections were rectangular and some were circular. Finally, on one of the panels of the polygon, he drew a perfect circle and, switching colors, he painted it gold.

The realization and the shock it caused hit me almost simultaneously. I sucked in a breath. Without thinking, I reached out and grabbed his arm and turned to look at him.

"Oh my god," I said. "Oh my god. You found the Voyager 2. You found the golden record!"

My hand was touching the bare skin of his forearm. I suddenly realized this when I saw the expression on Tulq'on's face. I wondered what emotions he was sensing from me at that moment. Did he feel my excitement, my awe, my wonder?

Did he feel how my heart skipped a beat as the shock slowly wore off and I was left to drown in his eyes?

His emotions were different than mine. What he'd told me was not new information to him, after all. His feelings were warmer: fond and affectionate, happy almost, yet still tinged with that anxiety and worry. I couldn't guess why he was feeling fond and happy at a time like this but figuring it out was not a priority at the moment.

It could have been the excitement of these new revelations. It could have been my sudden, overwhelming desire that he feel nothing but positive sensations in that moment. But suddenly I pushed forward towards him until my lips touched his.

It was tentative at first. I momentarily worried that I'd gotten it wrong and overstepped. But then his large, strong hand cupped the back of my head and he pulled me closer to deepen the kiss. I was hit with an onslaught of emotions; his mixed with mine until I could not tell which belonged to who. There was still the warmth and affection, but there was also the overwhelming heat of desire. The yearning for something more. The hope.

After a moment, the kiss gentled again and became almost reverent. The sensation of being bombarded with too many emotions lessened as I adjusted. And soon I was left with one thought.

I had kissed him. I was kissing Tulq'on. And it was everything.

Seven

Plans

DAVON

A short time later, after finding the strength to tear myself away from Tulq'on, I made my way to the control room to update the rest of the crew. After explaining the way we managed to communicate—still leaving out the empathic link, of course—I gave them the basics of what I'd discovered.

"So, from what I gather, this command ship wants to destroy us, and Tulq'on came here to protect us."

"Are they still coming for us?" Ledoux asked.

"I'm not sure. He understands more English than I ever would have guessed at this point, but it's still a bit of a process to communicate, so I wanted to let you all know what I've discovered so far," I said. "I think it would be safe to assume that they are, though. Maybe we can take action to protect ourselves."

"Like what?" Massey asked. "We're the first exploration ship with a live crew to make it this far, and we certainly didn't expect to meet other intelligent life within our own solar system. We have nothing to defend ourselves with."

"Maybe we can hide the Explorer 2," said Ledoux. "We can make sure Triton or Neptune are always between us."

"We're out here floating in space," Hayes said. "They could come at us from any direction. Not to mention how much more maneuverable their ships are compared to ours."

"Well," Ledoux responded, obviously trying to work out a solution as she spoke, "they're using the Kuiper Belt to help hide themselves from us, right? They are likely to appear to one side or the other of the Belt's plane, and probably within a close enough distance to take us by surprise. I can use that data to postulate the best likely spot to position the ship. Then we can leave a probe in our previous position to send us readings when the command ship is close enough and we can adjust our position as needed."

"That isn't going to buy us a whole lot of time," Hayes said.

"True, but hopefully it will give us time to come up with something more solid," Ledoux said.

"Do you think you can come up with something we can use as a weapon, Hayes?" Captain Boyton asked.

Hayes thought for a moment, no doubt mentally inventorying all the equipment and materials we had on hand.

"I may be able to," he answered. "I'll go now and start working on it."

"Captain," I said. My voice betrayed my concern.

"Don't worry, Pax. We'll only use it as a last resort. We'll try to find a peaceful solution first. We have one of their people on board, so maybe we can use him as a bargaining chip."

It rankled me to hear Tulq'on spoken of as an object to be bartered or a hostage, but then something more disturbing struck me.

"Unless they see him as a traitor now and think he's expendable." Just the thought made me break out in a cold sweat.

"Well, I guess you'd better get back to work on gathering more intelligence," Captain Boyton said.

I nodded and turned to head back to the medical bay.

"Wait," Massey said, stopping me with a hand on my arm. "Come to the mess hall first. I have some food and water put aside for you and your guest. I'm sure he must be hungry by now."

He probably was, but I hadn't thought to ask him. Guess I wasn't much of a host.

"Okay." I followed her to the mess while the others went off to take care of their various tasks. Once we were inside alone, Massey turned to me.

"So, you and our guest seemed to be getting along well."

"I guess so, yes. I mean, I think it's important to foster positive relations when encountering intelligent alien life for the first time, don't you?" I was trying to act casual, but I couldn't help but think back to the kiss. Yep, positive relations.

"Yeah, but like, really well. Well enough to make a little green monster show up to keep Hayes company."

I huffed at the idea. "I doubt very much Hayes feels jealous. More likely that he sees me as a toy he doesn't want to share. It really pisses me off when he acts all possessive like that. I mean, there is not, never has been, and never will be anything between us."

"I'm thinking he felt pretty confident he could change your mind and doesn't like that he now has competition." She turned to gather some rations and water as she continued to speak. "You and... sorry, how do you say his name again?"

"Tulq'on."

"Right, Tulq'on. You and he seem to be getting pretty close already. He's been here less than a day."

"Wow, less than a day? It seems like so much longer than that."

"That's my point, though. Are you sure he's not, I don't know, manipulating you somehow?"

I pursed my lips and studied Tira. I'd known her for years now and she was one of the good ones. She was the best. So, I decided to take a chance.

"Well, there is something. I haven't told the others because it seems personal somehow."

"You know you can tell me."

"I do," I replied. I took a deep breath. "Tulq'on is an empath."

Her brows shot up almost to her hairline. "He's a what, now?"

"He's an empath. He can share his emotions through touch and, judging by his reactions, he can sense mine as well." I waited for her reaction, expecting shock, disbelief—something of that nature. And she did look taken aback. For a minute, maybe.

Then, one side of her mouth quirked up and one brow lifted. "Through touch, you say. Hmm. That's very interesting."

I could feel my neck and face fill with heat. "Shut up," I mumbled. "I found out accidentally while I was examining him."

"Oh yeah, sure, sure. That makes sense." She was still smirking.

I couldn't stop myself from grinning even as I rolled my eyes at her.

"Just give me the food and let me—"

I was abruptly cut off by the sound of shouting from down the hallway. Massey and I looked at each other with fearful expressions, then we bolted out of the room and down the hallway to the source of the noise.

I ran in a panic toward the medical bay, where the shouting had originated from.

"What is it? What happened? Are they here?"

Captain Boyton looked at me with a concerned expression. "Hayes says he found Tulq'on messing with the control console."

There was one of these main consoles in the control room, one in the engineering room, and one here in the main room of the medical bay. I looked over to the far wall where it was located and, sure enough, there was a holographic screen open and the cover was ripped off one of the panels, exposing the components beneath. I sensed movement behind me and turned to see Tulq'on move into the doorway of his patient room. He looked at me with a concerned, questioning expression.

I turned back to Hayes.

"He ran back in there when I caught him. Probably trying to play innocent." Hayes fidgeted under my gaze.

My voice was low and menacing when I spoke. "You are a fucking liar." I hated that Hayes could work me up to the point of cursing, every time.

Hayes's expression morphed to one of hurt and betrayal. "You'd believe a stranger, an alien, over me?"

"Believe you over him? Seriously? He can't even defend himself! He doesn't speak enough of our language. He probably doesn't even understand what's going on right now; that you're accusing him of trying to sabotage our ship. And why would he even do that after risking his life to save us?"

Hayes's face turned to a sneer in a flash. The speed of the change was almost enough to leave me with whiplash. "You just don't want to believe that your boyfriend is not as great as you think he is."

"No, what I don't want to believe is that your petty jealousy caused you to forget that we're in a life or death situation here. An alien ship could be arriving at any time to blow us out of existence, and you're wasting our time with your games. And worse, if we'd believed you, it could have started a war with a technologically superior race of beings. Is all that worth it to you, Hayes?"

Now, he looked worried.

"Forgot that, did you? All of this," I gestured between us, then between myself and Tulq'on, "will mean absolutely nothing if there's nothing left of us but dust particles floating through space, you selfish son-of-a-bitch. For too long, I've put up with you treating me like some sort of possession for the sake of keeping the peace when we were never even together as a couple. And even if we were, you still wouldn't have the right to behave that way."

For a moment, he looked bewildered. I felt a spark of hope that he would admit what he'd done and apologize, but it was quickly dashed when something dark flashed in his eyes.

"Okay, sure. That may be true. But you'd fit with me better than you'd fit with him. At least I'm human. He's...he's blue!" He swept his hand up and down, indicating all of Tulq'on.

"Are you kidding me right now?" I was flabbergasted. "Did you not take the history and civics lessons the rest of us had to take as children? Did you not learn the dark history of humankind? Or did you sleep through those classes?

"You know, earlier today when Tulq'on told me that the command ship wants to destroy us, I argued that humankind had worked hard to improve. That we were so much better than our species had been in the past. That we deserved a chance." I shook my head. "Was I wrong about that?"

For the briefest moment he looked as though someone had slapped him, like he hadn't realized what he'd insinuated. But he apparently wasn't ready to give up quite yet. He reminded me of someone hanging off a cliff, scrambling to grab whatever crack or crevice they could hang on to so they wouldn't plummet to their death on the rocks below.

"Are you going to believe them over me, Captain?" he asked. "I mean, he's an alien we've only just met," he said, gesturing to Tulq'on, "and Davon is clearly infatuated."

"He doesn't have to believe me," I said. Everyone looked at me with curious expressions.

I walked over to Tulq'on and reached my hand out to him. He took it without hesitation. I immediately felt his confusion about what was happening, but it quickly changed to concern, bordering on anger, when he felt my swirling emotions. I led Tulq'on over to the Captain and started to lift his hand. I turned and met Tulq'on's deep, dark eyes.

"Okay?" I asked. He gazed at me questioningly for a moment, then nodded his head.

"Captain?" I prompted, bringing Tulq'on's hand up so it looked like he was offering a handshake. The captain barely hesitated before bringing his hand up to clasp Tulq'on's.

"What's going on?" Hayes demanded. "Is he doing some kind of manipulation trick or something?"

"Tulq'on is an empath, asshole," Massey said. I fought the sudden urge to laugh. She and Ledoux had been silent observers through this exchange, so to hear her utter those words right now helped to loosen some of the tension I'd been feeling.

I watched the captain's face as his expression drew tight, his lips pressed together and his jaw ticked. He nodded to Tulq'on and let his hand drop. Then he turned and nodded to me.

As he passed Hayes on the way out, he stopped and said, "You'd better pray that this time you've just wasted doesn't cost us our lives. Now get to work. You have a job to do. I don't want any more delays."

Eight

Closer

DAVON

The next evening, I awoke in some confusion, not sure where I was but feeling warm, comfortable, and secure. I lifted my head and looked up, then couldn't stop the smile that spread wide across my cheeks.

I was lying with my head on Tulq'on's chest, my arm thrown over his waist, and one leg slung across his. We'd been continuing to work on learning to communicate with each other and finding enough common ground that he could give me more details about what was going on. We'd plowed away at it since everyone left the previous afternoon. We'd worked for almost twenty-four hours straight when my eyes started to close of their own volition. I must have fallen asleep, and he'd apparently reclined the back of his bed until it was flat and let me use him as a pillow.

And what a fine pillow it was, too. I was not complaining.

Unable to stop myself, I let my hand wander over the planes of his chest. I had no idea if this kind of physique was normal for his kind or if, like humans, they varied a lot in their builds. His muscles were thick and firm—magnificent, really. Between his build and his height, I felt almost petit against him, though that had never been a term I would have used to describe myself in the past. I took care of myself and had my fair share of muscle, but it was nothing compared to him.

I looked up at his face and felt my cheeks flush when I realized he was watching me.

"Sorry," I said, and I started to pull my hand away. But he caught it in a gentle grip and placed it back on his chest, over his heart. I was pretty sure it was beating faster than it had been the last time I checked him over. With his free hand he shifted me until I was laying stretched out over his body. His eyes met mine for a moment, searching, as if to seek permission, then he lifted his head until his lips touched mine.

Our kisses started out soft and exploring as we learned one another's likes. Then our hands got involved. We ran them slowly over each other's bodies, memorizing the planes and valleys, finding the spots that made the other moan. Before long, I had my hands buried in his hair, pulling his head toward me as I kissed him like it was our last day together. And who knew? Maybe it was.

That thought sent a spike of sadness through me, and I knew he could feel it. We both knew we were on borrowed time here.

Soon, his ship would come and it would either turn us into space debris or Tulq'on would succeed in talking them into sparing us, in which case he would go back to his ship, we would continue our mission, and we would never see each other again.

We both tightened our embrace at the same time. Our kisses became more urgent, our tongues dancing, exploring.

I'm not sure who started it, but soon we were grinding against each other through our clothes. He held me close with one hand against my back as he rolled his hips against mine. His other hand drifted down to cup my ass through my pants, then it was inside on my bare skin, kneading and squeezing and using it as leverage to bring us close together as we rutted against each other.

It was embarrassing how quickly my balls drew up tight, but he was the hottest male I had ever met. Throw in on top of that that—both physically and emotionally—I could feel his desire for me, his need, and his affection, and I was a goner. My body started to shake with the effort of holding back, but then his movements became faster, more urgent, and less coordinated, and I knew he was close too. So, I let go, moaning into his mouth as I released inside my pants. Through our clothes, I could feel his cock jerk against mine at almost the same time, causing my orgasm to go on longer. We both came down slowly, holding each other tight and panting.

He kept his arms secured around me, so I lay there on top of him, spread out like a blanket, until the wetness in my pants cooled and grew uncomfortable. I slowly lifted myself off him, looking down to see that both of our clothes were stained with wet spots. I let out an embarrassed laugh and looked at him. Luckily, I had some clean patient suits in a cupboard nearby.

"I'm going to get us some fresh clothes to wear, then we can shower and wash these," I explained, using gestures to help.

"Okay," he said.

I smiled at him. He was amazing. He had learned so much of the language, so fast, it was just incredible. He was intelligent and hot, and I felt like I had hit the jackpot. Even if it could only be temporary, I was determined to appreciate it while I had it.

I gave him another little kiss, jumped up to gather what we needed, and came back to take his hand and drag him after me to the bathroom.

🐧 💜 🐧 💜 🐧

Tulq'on and I worked into the next day. About mid-way through the afternoon I asked the captain and the rest of the crew to join us for an update on what we knew.

"Tulq'on is learning English unbelievably fast, but he still understands more than he is comfortable speaking. So, I will go over what we know or suspect will happen, and Tulq'on can fill in anything I miss." I turned to him and he nodded his approval.

"First of all, Tulq'on thinks we should abandon the idea of making weapons," I started.

"What?" Hayes's question was almost a shout. "Are you kidding? We would be sitting ducks!"

"I know, but the Kyphomi Command already thinks we're dangerous. That's what they're called, by the way. Kyphomi. They see us as little more than warmongers and murderers out to destroy each other and our planet. We want them to see that we're different than what their intelligence and our history suggest."

"Also," Tulq'on chimed in, "you see my ship, yes?"

"We did," Captain Boyton responded.

"It is small, and it was hit. Then I crashed. Only small dent one side. Me, I am alive. Command ship is much bigger, much stronger."

"The point is," I added, "there is nothing on this ship that we can make a weapon with that has enough power to even damage the command ship."

"Why don't you let the engineer make that call?" Hayes asked. "For all we know, he might have been sent here to get us to let our guard down." He jabbed an index finger in Tulq'on's direction.

"Okay," Tulq'on said. "Use my ship target to practice. You will see."

"So what do you suggest we do, then?" Ledoux asked. "Just do nothing and let them destroy us?"

"No," I said. I took a deep breath. I wasn't too pleased with this next part of the plan. "So, from what Tulq'on has told me, his suit links him to the command ship. It's how they communicate, how they keep track of where he is, and how they track his physical condition. Right now, he isn't wearing it, so they will likely assume that he's dead.

"Tulq'on sacrificed himself and his ship in the hopes that it would make them reconsider their decision. To try to see what he saw in us. But there's no guarantee of that. They don't like to leave any traces of themselves behind, though, so they will come here to get the ship, at the very least. There's a chance they will come, blow us to bits, pick up their ship, then go on their way again."

"That's very comforting," Ledoux quipped.

"Well, the fact that we brought Tulq'on back to our ship will work to our advantage. They don't like to leave their people behind, either. So, he wants to put his suit back on so they know he's alive and on our ship. He doesn't think they will fire on us if they know he is here."

"How sure of that is he?" Captain Boyton asked.

"Yeah, how do we know they won't see him as a traitor and be happy to end him right along with us?" Hayes asked.

I glanced at Tulq'on. "I'm not sure. He wouldn't tell me." I narrowed my eyes at him, knowing he would understand. "But he did seem pretty certain it would hold them off for long enough to try to negotiate with them."

Everyone was quiet. The captain stood with his hands on his hips, chewing his bottom lip and looking at the floor.

"Okay, fine," he said at last. "We'll halt work on the weapon—"

"But—" Hayes started, but the captain raised a hand to silence him.

"But," Boyton echoed, "we will continue with our plan to hide the ship. At the very least, we'll be able to buy a little time."

He looked at Hayes. "Gather what you'll need, Hayes, just in case, but don't assemble anything."

That concession seemed to calm Hayes some. He nodded.

"I also think we need to get back to some normalcy instead of just sitting here waiting for the worse to happen," Captain Boyton said. "Let's assume we'll need to finish our mission. Massey and Ledoux, I want you to keep gathering samples and fuel from Triton and Neptune until it's time to make a move."

"Yes Captain," they said at the same time.

"At least we'll have some useful data to send back to Earth before...if the worst happens," Ledoux said.

"That reminds me," Boyton said, "as soon as you've gathered what you need, Hayes, I want you to come up with a plan to fix our long-distance communications array. Try to figure something out. Now the three of you," he continued, addressing Hayes and the two women, "get going."

He turned to Tulq'on and I. "Look," he said, "you two do what you need to do, but try to stay as safe as you can. Understand?"

"Yes sir," I said, smiling at his concern.

"We will try," Tulq'on added.

When the captain left, Tulq'on and I got back to work trying to learn each other's languages. He was immensely better at it than I was. But we had to do as much as we could before the command ship got here, because there was a possible next step to the plan that we hadn't mentioned yet.

Nine

Arrival

TULQ'ON

When my people are born, we have no control over our emotions: how strong we feel them, who we share them with. It is why we wear clothing that covers most of our skin. Most important of all, we always wear gloves. Yet, I had not put mine back on since I first removed them so Davon could examine my injuries. I have not wanted to. I liked that he could read me when we touched, though it did not seem to be anywhere near the extent that my people could.

As my kind grew, we learned more and more control until we knew how to shield our emotions, choosing what we wanted to share and with whom. We also learned to block out others' emotions so they could not be forced upon us. Those older and more practiced, however, could glean when someone was shielding, though very rarely could they feel the emotions themselves. By the time we have reached maturity we have mastered the skill of shielding so well it has become almost automatic.

If we wished to pair with another and we found someone with like interests, we shared ourselves little by little as we got to know each other. It was only when we were deciding whether to make it a complete pairing for the long run that we opened ourselves up completely. It was essential at that point to ensure compatibility.

These humans were like new-born babes. I could sense the stronger of their emotions just being in the room with them. But on that first day, I was dazed from the crash and I did not expect these humans to have any kind of empathic ability, or any ability to link with my kind. So, I neither shielded nor blocked emotions at that time. Then, when I touched Davon's bare hands with my own, I was completely taken aback. He was completely unshielded, and I could feel everything.

Davon was everything I'd longed for but never dared hope to find. He was beautiful, inside and out. Even when he was angry with that obsessed male, I could still sense the undercurrents of sympathy and sadness. It is not surprising the male wanted him so badly. One of the females wanted him as well, but it was clear she was trying to channel those feelings into care and friendship. I respected her for that.

I glanced down at Davon where he slept with his head upon my chest. Again. It made me smile. How lucky was I that a being as good, as caring, as hopeful, and as pure as he would return my feelings? Even in the face of coming danger, he still had an enthusiasm for life, boundless curiosity, and a sense of wonder at the universe that surrounded us.

I considered him as I idly stroked his hair. What did those others—those who could not sense emotions as I could—see when they looked at him? Could they see all these things that made him so special?

Yes, I am certain they could. They may not be able to explain it, but I am certain they would sense that there was something special about him. It was no mystery to me why he was desired by others. It was no mystery to me why I desired him as I had desired no other.

We had only recently met but we bonded so quickly. I have heard others speak of this happening but, until now, I never believed. It would break me when I had to give him up. I wished more than anything that I could keep him with me forever, but I knew that would be impossible. But if keeping him alive also meant losing him, then it was a price I was willing to pay.

Without thinking, I squeezed him tight, anticipating that time when I would no longer be able to do so. The action woke him. His eyes fluttered open, looking up until they settled on my face. I took the hand that rested on my chest and moved it down, then slid it back up underneath my shirt. I wanted his bare hand on my skin. I wanted him to know what I was feeling.

Perhaps it was selfish of me. Perhaps it was even cruel to let him know how I longed for him—burned for him—when I knew we could not have a future together. But I could not help wanting to take the time we did have and make the most of it.

I could tell when he felt it. His hand clutched against me and his eyes burned with the same intense desire that I felt. He got up onto his knees and then straddled me, pushing his other hand up under my shirt as well. I sat up to allow him to pull it off me, then I did the same to his shirt.

As soon as that barrier was out of the way, his lips were on mine and we were devouring each other. He pushed his body against mine and I pushed back, wanting to feel as much of his skin as I could, but this still was not enough. I pulled back for a moment so I could unfasten his pants. He slid off me long enough to push them all the way off, then he tugged at mine until they lay on the floor in a pile with his.

He swung his leg back over my hip and then our bodies were grinding against each other. He kissed me as though I was the air he needed to breath. He abruptly stopped and I groaned out a complaint. But then he leaned to the side to reach for something in the drawer of the table next to us. He opened the bottle and poured some of the substance into his hand. He leaned forward at the same time as he reached behind himself, and I finally understood what he was doing.

I did not think about it for long, though, before his lips were back on mine and he was intoxicating me with his kisses. He stretched and arched his back so he could reach behind himself and still reach to kiss me. I lifted my head towards him to help. He rolled his hips back and forth as he worked himself open, dragging his length against mine. He moaned into my mouth as he prepared himself for me, and it aroused me to the point that I wondered if I would hold out long enough to make him fully mine.

I got a chance to collect myself when he stopped moving momentarily to sit up and apply some of the slippery substance to my hard length. He looked at it wide-eyed for a moment and I felt his spike of fear that was quickly replaced with determination. Then he repositioned himself above me and began to sink down onto me. We both moaned when I breached his entrance and he paused to take some deep breaths. As soon as I felt his muscles loosen, he pushed himself further onto me. It took some time, but he continued slowly until he was fully seated and I was as deep inside of him as I could go. The feeling of his hot body wrapped around me was indescribable. I was close to finishing before we even began. But I held out.

We were soon moving in a steady rhythm, with Davon alternating from rocking his hips back and forth to leaning forward and lifting and lowering himself on me. I sat up so I could clutch him close to me as he drove us closer to the edge. The entire time, his lips were on mine. We were sipping at each other, sharing panted breaths. In that moment, we were one.

From time to time, my people did take part in this activity while keeping ourselves shielded when there was nothing but physical attraction between those involved. But what Davon and I were doing? Reveling in the physical sensations of our bodies moving together while opening our emotions fully to each other? This was the ultimate act of intimacy and trust for my people. I knew that allowing myself to emotionally link with him even more deeply like this would make it harder when the time came to part, but I could not stop myself. Not everyone got to experience this kind of connection in their lifetime, so I wanted to explore it fully while it was mine.

Soon, too soon, his body began to shake, then I felt the warmth of his seed hitting my chest and abdomen. As his inner muscles fluttered and tightened over my length, I lost my fight for control as well. I shouted out and pulled his body firmly against me as I filled him up and marked him as mine, just as he had marked me as his. Then we collapsed back on the bed.

We lay there holding each other, his forehead against my collar bone, as we caught our breath. I felt sadness creeping its way back in and I felt something wet hit my skin. I cupped Davon's face in my palms and lifted his head to look at him. He was crying, and I could feel his despair. I knew he was thinking about the time when we'd have to separate, just as I was. I brushed away a tear with my thumb. I was surprised when he had to do the same for me.

He pressed his lips gently to mine and, on a shaky breath, he whispered, "I love you."

I knew those words. I had searched them up, anticipating the time when I would get to say them to him. He did not need to voice them, of course. I felt his love emanating warmly, and forcefully, from him. But hearing them spoken aloud filled me with happiness, even as they broke my heart.

I returned his gentle kiss and whispered the words back against his lips. "I love you."

He dropped his face into the crook of my neck and I wrapped him tightly in my embrace, wishing with all that I had that I could find a way to keep him, and that he would want to keep me too.

They were here.

My people were here, and with their arrival came the knowledge that my time with the humans, my time with Davon, was soon coming to an end.

My hands shook as I toyed with the controls on the forearm panel of my suit. After Davon and I had proclaimed our love, we arose and bathed, and I donned this suit once again. It would read my life force and health, it would note my location, and the commander would know that I was alive and that I was here, on this ship. I clung to the hope that my presence would be enough to save the humans, but that hope was not enough to still the shaking of my hands.

I glanced over to where Davon sat in front of his holo-screen, watching from the medical bay as his captain maneuvered the ship so that the planet would be between it and the command ship. It would only buy them time until command decided to send out one of the smaller vessels. The human vessel was no match in speed or firepower.

The humans knew this of course. They matched my own people in intelligence, though they were behind us in advancements in technology. I had no doubt they would catch up if given the opportunity. This crew knew their ship was no match, but they had such a capacity for hope. I had seen this time and again in my study of the humans. And I knew they would cling to their hope until they were forced to give it up.

I approached Davon and he looked up at me.

"Are you ready?" I asked, holding my hand out to him. He nodded and placed his hand in mine. It was strange, feeling his emotions as muted as they were through my gloves when I'd become accustomed to feeling them fully.

I helped him stand, then pulled him to me as I leaned down and rested my forehead against his. Closing my eyes, I took a deep breath, taking in the scent of him. His warmth and affection wrapped around me, but it was tinged with the bitter sting of the pain of coming loss.

His emotions mirrored my own.

"Whatever happens," he whispered, "never forget that I love you. I love you and I always will."

I tilted my head to kiss him and tasted the salty tang of the tears that ran down his cheeks and over his lips. I wondered if he tasted mine too.

"I know, my heart. Time and space does not matter. You will live in here," I took his hand and placed it on my chest. "Always."

I kissed him again, keeping it soft and reverent.

Davon chuckled and wiped his tears with the back of his hand. "Okay, I think we need to pull ourselves together before we go out there." We held on to each other for a few more moments as we tried to get our emotions under control. Then it was time to go.

We had decided that we would go to the control center of the Explorer 2 when it was time for me to contact the commander. That way, the entire crew could be kept apprised of what was happening while keeping an eye on their cameras, windows, screens, and sensors. Clear communication between all could mean the difference between life and death.

Davon clung to my hand as we walked, and this pleased me very much.

When we arrived, I went to one of the computing terminals to tie in my communications device. We would be unable to see command, but we would hear them. Of course, the humans would not understand my language as we spoke, but I would be there with the crew to let them know should I discover the command ship was going to do anything. These humans were trusting in me and it was a great responsibility, and a great honor.

Once I was linked in, I looked at the crew and nodded. Then I sent my signal to the commander.

Ten

Meeting

TULQ'ON

Tulq'on," the commander addressed me in our Kyphomi
language. "You have much to answer for."

"I feel no regret."

"You must return to deal with the repercussions of your
actions."

"I will gladly return, if you can give me assurances that the
humans will not be harmed and that this vessel will be left in
peace."

"You are in no position to make demands, Tulq'on."

"I believe I am in a very good position. I am here on this ship,
and I will not leave it until you give me your word they will be
unharmed."

"You have defied orders. Are you so sure that we would not
destroy the ship and you along with it?"

"Am I certain? No. But I would hope that would be the case...Father."

"And you would be willing to put your life at risk for them? For creatures who have fought and killed each other over differences within their own species? How do you think they will behave once they learn there are others out here, others who are much more different?"

"I am certain you know what my answer would be. Tell me, Commander, why was I assigned to study them if your decision had already been made?"

"It was not but, as you know, the situation has changed."

"Many things have changed, Commander, including the humans. I have gathered the intelligence to prove their kind has made immense improvements. Does that count for nothing? Or does the fact that we have allies in need of a new home planet make it count for nothing?"

"My son, you are basing your belief in them on what is a very short time when compared to the amount of time they spent warring and damaging their planet. There is no guarantee they will stay on this new path. They do not deserve to keep what they would destroy."

"You know, the humans have a word unlike any of ours. It is irony." I felt the surprise of the human crew members when they heard me speak a word they recognized. "It is the greatest irony of our people that we are empaths, yet we can be so cold and unfeeling. There is a whole species of beings on Earth, and our leaders decide that they do not deserve the planet that birthed them. Our leaders think that the solution is to destroy the humans and hand over the planet to allies whose own planet is on the verge of collapse. But who are we to make such a decision? Who are you to make it? I cannot help but wonder if my advice would have been heeded if we did not have that alliance to benefit from."

"You know it was not my decision alone."

"Do you think that makes it better? When I crashed on that moon," I said, "these humans rescued me from my damaged ship. Do you know what the human physician felt when he saw me?"

"I would presume it was fear, and we have seen what their past actions have been when they have been faced with the fear of that which they do not know."

"You are both correct and incorrect. Yes, he felt fear, but underneath that was worry and concern, not the panic one would expect. It was that worry and concern that caught my attention, even through the haze of semi-consciousness. It caused me to turn my head toward him. And once I did that, his fear disappeared, and he was filled with relief. Do you see, Father? The fear he felt was not of me. It was for me. He feared for my life."

"It is doubtful you would have died from such a crash." His tone was dismissive. It annoyed me greatly.

"They did not know that. They did not know me, yet they brought me to their ship to care for me."

The commander was quiet for a moment, and I could hear whispered voices in the background. No doubt it was the other members of the command group weighing in. I took this opportunity to look at Davon. The concern he was feeling was etched in his expression. It must be difficult for all of them to have their lives hang in the balance and not understand what was being said. I took Davon's hand and gave it a gentle squeeze before letting it drop again.

This particular human amazed me. He had not even known about the existence of other intelligent life until a few days ago. Now, here his crew was, at the mercy of an alien command and their larger, more powerful vessel, and Davon's concern was still for me—a member of the species that threatened them. A warmth filled me up almost to bursting. I had never met another being like him, and chances were I never would again.

Finally, my father addressed me again. "If you want a chance to prove the humans have changed, then bring me the physician you spoke of. We will test him and make a judgment."

It was my turn to fear now. I did not want him on the command vessel. There would be no guarantee he would leave there in safety. I was tempted to offer Hayes in his place, but I was fairly certain that would spell doom for humankind.

"I do not think that is a good idea," I hedged.

"Let me state this in clearer terms, Tulq'on. You will either bring me the human, or we will destroy their ship and pluck you from the debris. The humans would not survive, of course, but there is a chance you would, however small that chance may be."

I did not doubt he would do as he said. I did not need to feel his emotions; I could hear the determination in his voice. I looked at Davon, and I was glad he was not touching me in that moment. He did not need to share my fear and anxiety.

"They want to meet you," I said in English.

"Me?" His eyes widened in concern. "Why?"

"They want to test you."

Apparently, those were not the best words to use, because there was an immediate spike of panic.

"What kind of test?" he asked.

"They will ask you questions and they will read your emotions as you respond."

He took in a deep breath and let it out. "Well, that doesn't sound too bad." He gave me a little smile. "I will do whatever you need me to do."

I would not tell him what was at stake with the test. He had many matters to worry about and did not need this one added.

I nodded to Davon and responded to the commander in Kyphomi.

"He will come." Of course he would. He would always do what was necessary, and there really was no other choice.

Davon and I used the Explorer 2's lander to get to the command ship, since there was no way for one of our smaller vessels to dock with theirs. Davon was surprisingly calm. After my conversation with the commander, the human male had insisted on holding my hand almost non-stop. His inability to read my emotions during that time had left him a little shaken. The only time he let me out of his reach was when Hayes had come to speak with him.

They had gone to stand a short distance away from me to talk, at Hayes's insistence. I could still hear them, of course, and they did not bother to hush their voices. Hayes did not realize how much English I had come to learn in the short amount of time I had been there, and Davon wanted me to hear in case he needed assistance.

Also, I could feel the emotions in the room quite clearly. To give Hayes credit, he did truly care for Davon, even if it bordered on an unhealthy obsession. He apologized to Davon for his behavior and, when he could not convince Davon to stay on board the Explorer 2, he implored him to be careful.

I had underestimated Davon. He knew exactly what was at stake even if I had not given him the words, and he was resolved to follow this through and do his best to save his people. He did not feel confident in his ability to do so, but he was determined to try.

Now, as we made our way down long corridors toward the Command Center with one guard leading us and two others behind, I still did not feel any fear coming from him. There was frustration, which—from the way his hand kept twitching toward mine—I guessed was due to him not knowing how I was feeling. There was anxiety from him as well, of course, but it was often interrupted by awe and excitement whenever we passed by anything that was foreign to him, which was almost everything. This male continually surprised me with his reactions.

I glanced around, trying to see the ship from his perspective. The Explorer 2 was quite bare and utilitarian, carrying only the necessities. The Kyphomi Command Ship must look luxurious to him. The hallways were dark, curved and lit with faint blue light that pulsed in lines along the walls like blood through veins in living flesh.

"You have noticed the ways in which my eyes differ from your own, yes?" I asked the question quietly. The guards could not understand English, but I still felt as though my conversations with him should be just for us.

Davon looked up and met my gaze. The corner of his mouth lifted in an affectionate smile. "Of course," he responded.

"Kyphomi do not need as much light to see as humans. That is why the lighting is muted in comparison to your ship."

"Oh," he said. "I thought they were trying to set an intimate mood."

I gave a little smile at his attempt to lighten a tense time with humor. I reached out to give his fingers squeeze before releasing them again. I was still wearing my suit with the gloves attached. We could shield our emotions and block out others most of the time, but it was much harder to do when there was skin-to-skin contact, so we wore gloves to avoid accidental or unwanted intrusions.

The Command Ship was shaped much as my smaller vessel had been: It was pointed at the very front and smoothed into an ever-widening curve until it got to the back, where it ended in a crescent shape. The command center was located at the highest point, but from the outside you could see no windows or screens. It looked a sleek, uniform black. But once inside, you could notice that there were, in fact, many windows. We could see out clearly enough, but others could not see in. They could not even tell that we had windows.

As we reached the large double doors that were the entrance to the Command Center, the lead guard tipped his staff weapon to knock twice with the end. After a moment, both doors swung wide. I took a deep breath to ensure my emotions were calm, thus less easy to sense, then I walked towards the imposing figure that stood in the center of the room, his black robe flowing down to his feet. We were no more than 10 arms' lengths away when the guards stopped us. The commander took off a glove and held out a hand to me, palm up.

Stepping forward a few paces, I took off the glove on that side and placed my bare hand in his. Then I waited.

My father was one of the oldest and strongest Kyphomi, which meant that his ability to read emotion was strong. He could not only read what one was feeling at that moment, but he could also go back a short distance in time.

"I see," he said. "This one?" He indicated Davon with a nod of his head.

"Yes, Commander."

"Well, it looks like you will be punished no matter what we decide to do. The pain of lost love can be quite unbearable at times. I can only imagine how it will feel for you when we depart and you must leave him behind." He glanced at Davon. "I do not need touch to read him." He tilted his head as he considered Davon. "He worries for you, and for his people."

I did not say anything in response. My father was not an uncaring man. He just put his duty as commander ahead of all else.

"I cannot say I expected this," he said. "Though you did not either." There was just the slightest hint of amusement in his voice. He was shielding his emotions, though, so I could not know for certain what he was really feeling.

"Let us sit," he said, and turned to walk to a small room off to the left of the main room. Inside, another two members of command were already sitting. My father arranged us so that he was sitting at one side of the table with the sub-commander named Za'ko between him and I, another sub-commander, named Tak'ir, across from me, and Davon directly across from my father.

Davon was feeling uncomfortable and suspicious, which was not surprising. So far since he had come aboard the command ship, the only words spoken in his language were when I had spoken to him about the lighting.

"Tulq'on," my father began, "I will ask questions of your human, and you will translate them as closely as you can. If you deviate from the intentions of the question, Za'ko will inform me, and it will not go well for you and your friend. You are always to leave your emotions completely unshielded. Do you understand?"

"Yes." Za'ko, in other words, would monitor my emotions and inform my father should he sense any signs of dishonesty. Not that he needed any help with that. It was just an extra precaution for when the questioner's attention was elsewhere.

"Tak'ir will moderate. He will be watching. If you say anything other than what I am asking you to translate, he will shoot you with his stunner and send your friend off thinking that you are dead. If you try to warn the human of this, if you try to touch him, Tak'ir will shoot you before you can think to act."

"I understand." My words were calm but I felt my anger building. It was quickly followed by frustration with myself for allowing them to sense my feelings. I was not permitted to shield, but they could not admonish me for staying calm in tense circumstances. I knew that was the correct action, but it was not easy in this moment.

I knew how these interrogations worked, though I had never witnessed any from my current perspective. I placed my bare left hand on the small table between us. Za'ko placed his hand atop mine. Then my father, the great Commander Sulik'ka, leaned forward to look me in the eye and said, "If we think he is a threat in any way, we will stun him, send him back to his ship, and follow through with our original plan."

I felt a spike of anger so strong it almost burst free. The only reason I was able to contain my temper was the knowledge that Davon would never do anything that could be looked upon as a threat. It was not in his nature. But I most certainly did not appreciate the threats my father was leveling at us. I was certain, though, that the fact that I was the commander's son made him feel obligated to be even harder on me than he would be on others. And as his son, I needed to pass his tests.

"Tell your friend to place his hand in the center of the table." I did as he asked, and when Davon placed his hand down, my father placed his on top. Then, the questioning began.

Eleven

Mis/Understanding

DAVON

The Kyphomi officers had been questioning me for what felt like hours, although there was nothing in the room that was familiar to me, so I didn't even know if they had a way to mark the passage of time.

At first it had been strange to be interrogated by Tulq'on, but I quickly realized that, even though Tulq'on translated, he most certainly was not the one asking the questions. There were times where he became angry or frustrated but held himself in check. I wasn't allowed to touch him, so I couldn't feel his emotions, but I could see those times when his jaw ticked, or his eyes narrowed, or his lips pressed tight together. I noticed when he had to take a deep breath or two before repeating a question to me.

I didn't care what they asked me. I would answer any question if it meant they would let my crew go free and if they would make Tulq'on's punishment for helping us light. No one should be punished for being good and noble.

They started out by asking me about my mission: Why were we out here? What were our intentions? What were our end goals? Was I important enough to know if our leaders had different intentions than stated for this mission?

Then they asked me very detailed questions about human history. I know Tulq'on mentioned he'd studied us, but I was not expecting them to have gone quite so in depth. I wanted to ask them how they managed to watch us closely enough to get this information without us noticing.

When they asked me about advancements in the last century, I automatically assumed they meant technological advancements. I did not get far in my explanation before they were clarifying. What they wanted to know about was the advancements in our political and social systems. In how we took care of our planet. What we planned to do to revive our planet and deal with the issues that had cropped up over the years, such as overpopulation.

That last one was a little easier to address. Over the last century or so, we had been subjected to a couple of natural disasters of nearly catastrophic proportions, including earthquakes, tsunamis as the ice caps melted, and pandemics. We had lost a significant portion of our world population, and it had never recovered to previous numbers.

But these questions were making me uneasy. Why did they want this type of information? What was their goal? Curiosity about other cultures and other species was natural—well, it was for humans, at least. But their questions were very specific and, I felt, leading.

"Tulq'on," I said. "What's going on? Why are they asking so many questions about Earth? Does this have to do with more than just my crew and the Explorer 2?" I was starting to feel panicked. "Are they going to do something to my planet? If this is because we know about you now, the captain hasn't been able to get messages out to Earth. You know that. What if we ... I don't know ... what if we promised not to tell anyone about you? Made an oath or something?" Even as I said it, I knew they would never agree. Why would they trust our word when they obviously didn't think humans as a species were trustworthy?

Tulq'on watched me carefully as I spoke, but he didn't say anything. He pressed his lips together and glanced at the guy sitting across from him, then looked back at me. He was tense. He shot me a look and shook his head. I couldn't be sure, but it looked like he was trying to warn me about something.

Tulq'on turned to look at the guy questioning me, who was introduced earlier as Commander Sulik'ka. He said something to him, and the man's response was one that Tulq'on apparently did not like. He became agitated and whatever it was he said next sounded irate. There was some back and forth that followed, and Tulq'on was clearly getting angrier and angrier. He stood up, gesturing toward me. The commander said something and tipped his head to the guy who sat directly across from Tulq'on. I looked over and was alarmed to see he was holding what looked like a weapon of some kind. Right now, though, he just held it casually, like he was reminding Tulq'on it was there.

The next few minutes happened very fast. Tulq'on raised his voice and turned away from the commander. He grabbed my hand and, yes, he was angry. Fuming. He moved to the door, pulling me behind him. I looked behind us and saw the guy with the weapon raise it and aim it at Tulq'on.

"No!" I yelled, and I threw myself between Tulq'on and the aggressor just as I saw a flash. I felt a sharp pain in the center of my torso.

"Davon!" I heard Tulq'on yell, then his strong arms were around me. That's the last thing I remember before everything went black.

🐧 ♥ 🐧 ♥ 🐧

I awoke slowly, my eyes fluttering open to a room accented with muted blue light. At first I did not remember where I was. I looked around slowly and it started to come back to me. I was on Tulq'on's Command Ship.

I felt a sudden shot of fear as I recalled Tulq'on being shot at. Almost as if my thoughts had made him materialize, he jumped up from where he'd been laying on the floor.

"Davon. What is wrong? Are you in pain?"

"Tulq'on," I breathed. "You're alive."

"I am." He kneeled beside me and placed his hand on my cheek.

"Wait. Why were you on the floor?"

"I needed to be near you to make sure you were okay."

I looked down at the bed I was laying on. There was plenty of room. "Why weren't you on here with me?"

"I did not want to hurt you."

He was still touching my face, though, so I knew it was more than that. I laughed. "How could you possibly be unsure of me, Tulq'on? Isn't it obvious by now what you mean to me?"

He lowered his hand. "You were shot by one of my people. They were not good to you when they asked questions. I thought maybe you changed your mind."

"Don't be ridiculous. I would never condemn an entire species based on the actions of a few." I reached for his hand and held it tightly. "What? What is that emotion you have right now?"

"I just...that was what my people were doing to yours. They were judging all humans based on the actions of some. I tried to tell them it was not the same as it had once been, but they did not listen. That is why I saved your ship." He shook his head. "You are...I do not have the words in English." Then he said something I could not understand. I'm pretty sure there were some sounds in there I couldn't even make.

"Is that a good thing?"

"It is the very best thing."

I tugged on his hand and scooted over and he climbed onto the bed with me. He leaned over me, staring down into my eyes.

"I cannot believe you're alive," I said. "I thought for a moment there that I'd never see you again. Wait. How am I alive?"

"The weapon they used is not to kill. It is to…" There was a pause as he struggled to find the right word. "It is to make unconscious."

"It was a stun gun?"

"Stun, yes. That is the word." Then he leaned down to place a soft kiss to my lips. "But, Davon, you are human. Much more fragile than Kyphomi people. I felt so much fear. I thought I would never get to speak with you again—never hold you close or feel you in here again." He placed his hand on his chest. "I do not think I could live if you did not."

I reached one hand up to wipe his tears as I used the back of my other hand to wipe my own from my cheeks.

"I'm here, my love." I wrapped my arms around him and pulled him close. "But what happened in there, Tulq'on? Why did everything suddenly get so volatile?"

"My father, he made a decision that was not his to make. He wanted to keep you on the ship and take you with us."

I felt a little spark of hope, then the shock of realization. Tulq'on sucked in a quick breath.

"What is it Davon? Why such pain and sadness? I talked to him. He said you can go." He shook his head. "I don't understand. Why does that make you more sad? You feel…hurt?"

I shook my head. "It's stupid."

"Please, tell me."

"It's just…" I glanced up at him then dropped my eyes. "You don't want me with you?"

He had been stroking my hair soothingly, so I felt his surprise at my question.

"Of course!" He said. "Of course I always want you with me. But he wished to force you to give up your life, your home, your family, your planet. He wanted you to give up everything, and he did not care what that would mean to you." He ran the backs of his large fingers down along my cheek bone. "I would keep you with me always if I could, but not if it meant forcing you to give up all that you love."

I laughed. I'm sure he knew how I was feeling, but he was looking at me with his brows drawn down and pulled together in confusion, like he didn't know why. I shook my head at him.

"You don't understand," I said. "Being out here in space, seeing the stars and planets up close and not through images taken from far off—this is what I've always dreamed of. If I could do this for the rest of my life, I would die a happy man." I reached up, cupped his cheek, and stared into his eyes.

"And there's another thing you don't seem to understand." He raised an eyebrow in question.

"There is nothing I love more than you."

It was true. How it had happened in such a short amount of time—out here in space where the only new things I thought I'd encounter were rocks, metals, and, with any luck, some single-celled organisms—I had no idea. But I felt it to the very core of my being.

He sucked in a breath as he took in the depth of my emotions, and then he was kissing me passionately. When we pulled apart enough to take in some air, I asked him, "How much privacy do we have in here?"

Twelve

Next Adventures

DAVON

Tulq'on answered my question by leaning in to kiss me deeply once again, while at the same time reaching down to pull my shirt up. I reached my hand up under the back of his as well and did the same to him. We paused our kisses just long enough to pull our shirts over our heads, then our lips met again. How we managed to get our pants off while locked onto one another I don't know, but soon enough we were both gloriously naked. Skin to skin with nothing between us but intense physical sensation and all-encompassing emotion.

I whimpered when his lips left mine, but soon they were traveling down along my body, worshiping every inch of me along the way. When his tongue touched my nipple, my body jerked, which caused me to let out a hiss of pain. It had hit quickly from where I'd been shot with the stunner, but it passed quickly as well. Tulq'on had started to pull back, but I grabbed his head, fingers threaded in his silky hair, and held him in place.

"Don't stop," I pleaded.

He continued his sensual exploration of my torso, dipping his tongue into my navel briefly, then continuing down. He teasingly bypassed the place I wanted his mouth, instead drawing his tongue down along the crease where leg meets groin. He kissed and nipped his way down along the inside of one thigh then back up the other. Then, finally, he licked a thick stripe up the center of my shaft. I let out a shout as I felt his warm mouth wrap around me. He sucked and licked along my length, taking me deep, then pulling back to tease the tip before starting the tortuous process over again.

"Please," I begged him. "Please. I need you."

He lifted his head and met my eyes. "I do not have any of the thing you used."

"Lube?" I asked, and he nodded.

"My people are stronger than yours. We do not need such things."

"Give me your hand," I said. "I have an idea."

He did as I asked and I sucked two of his fingers into my mouth. I rolled my tongue over them, getting them slick with my saliva. When they were nice and wet, I said, "Work me open."

I felt his flush of desire at my request, and it deepened my own. He rubbed a wet fingertip around the outside of my entrance, toying with it until it relaxed some. I moaned as he breached me. He took his time playing and exploring. He sucked and licked at me just enough to tease, adding another finger each time I begged for more until he had three of them inside of me.

The feeling of his digits moving inside me while being bombarded with his desire and lust made me feel wanton. I writhed on his fingers until I felt like I would perish if I didn't get him inside me. He groaned, lust surging once more.

"Come up here," I said, grabbing his hair and tugging gently. He seemed unsure of what I wanted, so I grabbed the globes of his ass and pulled him up towards my head until he was close enough for me to take his cock in my mouth.

At this time I was too turned on to have much patience or finesse, especially given his size, but that was fine because I needed this to be sloppy and messy.

"Davon," he gasped before long, "too close."

I let him go with a pop. "I need you inside me."

He didn't hesitate. He had played with me to the point where I was relaxed and loosened and that, coupled with my saliva, helped ease the way as he breached me. Still, I couldn't help but to cry out as he stretched me open with this thick girth. He paused and I took a few deep breaths. Then I grabbed his ass and bore down as I guided him in as deep as he could go. I knew I would feel him for days, but I welcomed that. I wanted to feel the reminder that he was mine and I was his after believing I would have to give him up.

He paused, taking deep slow breaths to calm himself, then he leaned down with his body over mine, elbows by my head supporting his weight and fingers in my hair. I had thought the sex was going to be crazy and desperate. Instead he slowed down. He looked into my eyes as he began to move, and no words were needed between us. He practically poured the depth of his feeling into me, and that same love and sense of home was reflected in his eyes as he moved inside me. It was almost too much.

I reached up and wrapped a hand around the back of his neck and pulled him in for a kiss. As we both flew higher and higher we were no longer kissing, but our lips still touched as we panted our breaths into one another. I felt my orgasm building and building until I was right on the edge, without ever having to touch myself. I barreled right over just as Tulq'on's mouth closed over mine again, catching my shout of ecstasy as he slammed into me once, twice more, then held himself deep inside as he shuddered and twitched.

Once we had calmed enough and our breathing started to even out, Tulq'on pulled out. I groaned at the loss. He leaned over the bed and grabbed his shirt to clean us off, then he tossed it back to the floor and laid down beside me. I curled into him and rested my head on his chest.

We didn't speak as we lay there together. We just felt. And all there was between us in this perfect moment was love, simmering desire, warmth, and happiness.

So much happiness.

꙰ ♥ ꙰ ♥ ꙰

"Hi Mom. Hi Dad," I said as I looked into the camera to make a video message for them. The only family I had on Earth, but now not the only family I had in the universe.

"I have some news. I met someone." I laughed and shook my head. "I'll bet you're wondering how that happened out here at the edge of the solar system. It's a long story, but I'll try to keep it as short as I can."

I launched into the retelling of the events that led up to this point, though I decided to leave out the part where Tulq'on's father and the rest of the Kyphomi Command had wanted to exterminate all humans and give our planet to some friends of theirs. Like, here, we got something for you. What? No! It's not a re-gift. Pfft. No one has ever been here before.

And, of course, I also left out the sexy parts.

The way Tulq'on told the story to my crew, in his very good but imperfect English, I was the hero of the story. The savior of humankind. I thought he was a little too in love to see clearly.

He had risked his own life, gone against his leaders—including his own father—and took a chance of becoming an enemy to his own people to save us. Then he refused to leave our ship until they would hear him out. If those weren't the actions of a hero, I didn't know what were. Yet he credited my "jumping in front of him to keep him from getting shot" stunt as what finally led them to see that maybe there was hope for us after all. Enough hope, apparently, to give us a chance.

When I reminded him the weapon was just a stunner, his response was, "But you did not know that."

"So, the Kyphomi Command," I continued, "has asked me to come aboard their ship. They want me to teach them about our people and our planet, and to teach them the language. Of course, I'll have to learn Kyphomi too." I laughed. "Then I'll know English, Spanish, French, German, and Kyphomi. How is this my life?

"Anyway, the Kyphomi Command Ship has to find a home still for one of its allies." Hopefully an unoccupied one this time. "So, the Explorer 2 will likely get back to Earth before we do. They've given our crew some items and a message to bring back as a way of introducing themselves. They're hoping it will help pave the way and get our people used to the idea that there is, in fact, other intelligent life out here before they show up on our doorstep."

Tulq'on entered the room at that moment but hesitated by the door. I smiled and stretched out my hand to him. He walked over and took it, returning my smile.

"So, Mom, Dad, this is Tulq'on. In a couple of days, just before the Explorer 2 is set to leave, we'll be having a ceremony where we'll become..." I looked at Tulq'on then back at the camera, "Well, I haven't quite gotten the hang of how to say the word yet. But basically it's the Kyphomi equivalent of a wedding, where we'll become husbands." I felt a wave of happiness rush over me—probably from both of us. I turned and beamed at Tulq'on and he placed an arm over my shoulders and gave a little squeeze.

I looked back at the camera. "Remember, dad, our trips to all the different observatories when I was young? How I looked at all the pictures taken with probes and long-range equipment, looked at the planets and the stars through the telescopes, and I would tell you how I wanted to go there someday? This mission made that dream come true. And now—it seems unbelievable, even while I'm here living it—but now I will get to look out and see even more planets and stars with nothing but a window between us. Places we never even knew existed. I'll get to put on a suit and stand where no human has ever stood before.

"I'll get to see all the wonders our universe has to offer, and I'll get to see them with my own eyes and not through someone else's lens. And the most wonderful part of all? I will get to do all that with the love of my life by my side."

Thanks For Reading!

I hope you enjoyed reading
The Empath's Lover.

If you would be kind enough to leave a review
on Amazon or wherever you purchased the book,
it would help make a big difference to how
this book is represented in the algorithms. The
better represented it is, the easier it will be for
other readers to find it. **A huge thank you in
advance!**

Also By Sidonie Savage

The Empath's Second Chance: The Kyphomi Empaths Book 2

A human wounded by rejection. A kyphomi scarred by loss. Will they survive long enough to realize they are each other's second chance?

Sylas Hayes had only just learned that humans were not alone in the universe when he lost the man he pined for to an alien. Heartbroken, and distrusting of their new allies, Sylas decides that love is not worth the pain.

Ksa'in is the first kyphomi to serve on a human spaceship. One crewman catches his attention from the very start. But Sylas is reeling from a recent heartbreak, and Ksa'in is haunted by a past loss.

After Sylas is abducted by alien rebels, Ksa'in is determined to find him and bring him back where he belongs. Stranded on an inhospitable planet, they are forced to rely on one another to survive and with each new danger they face together, an unexpected bond begins to form. Will they find true love amidst the chaos or will the universe tear them apart?

If you enjoy MM Sci-Fi Romance, then you'll be captivated by this heart-pounding story of love and survival. Buy now before the price changes!

Content Warning: The Empath's Second Chance *is the second book in* The Kyphomi Empath's *series. It can be read as a standalone, but is best read with* The Empath's Lover. *It contains adult themes and language and explicit sexual content. It is intended for readers 18+.*

Get your copy here:

About the Author

S idonie Savage is a romance fanatic who enjoys many subgenres of romance, including fantasy, paranormal, sci-fi, contemporary, and LGBT+ (especially MM). She also enjoys watching BL series. Sidonie dreams of the day when all forms of love between consenting adults are accepted and appreciated.

A teacher and mom by day and an avid reader and writer by night, Sidonie has a B.A. in Language and Literature, a B.Ed., and a Graduate Certificate in Creative Writing.

<u>Follow Sidonie on Social Media:</u>

Website: www.sidoniesavage.com

Facebook: @SidonieSavageAuthor

Twitter: @SidonieSavage

Instagram: @sidonie_writes

Tiktok: @SidonieSavageAuthor